Dempsey, now wary at the thought of driving this sophisticated man in her cluttered car, stood for a moment as she opened the door and stared across at him waiting on the passenger side.

'I hope you're not one of those people who can't bear to be driven, Dr Saville,' she said firmly. 'I spend a lot of time in my car and know the area well, so I can't stand back-seat drivers.'

'I promise not to say a word. And the name is Bart.'

In the half-light, Dempsey could see a cheeky grin cross his face, and she got into the driver's seat and slammed the door, wondering if perhaps she'd bitten off more than she could chew.

Christine Adams is a registered nurse living in the West Country, who has worked for many years in the N.H.S. and still nurses part-time. She has been writing for some years, mainly short stories and articles. She finds the dramas and tensions in the medical world an ideal background in which to find plots and story-lines.

DEMPSEY'S DILEMMA

BY

CHRISTINE ADAMS

MILLS & BOON LIMITED
ETON HOUSE   18–24 PARADISE ROAD
RICHMOND   SURREY   TW9 1SR

First published in Great Britain 1992
by Mills & Boon Limited

© Christine Adams 1992

Australian copyright 1992
Philippine copyright 1992
This edition 1992

ISBN 0 263 77590 9

Set in 10½ on 12 pt Linotron Palatino
03-9203-48501
Typeset in Great Britain by Centracet, Cambridge
Made and printed in Great Britain

CHAPTER ONE

DEMPSEY edged her small red car against the kerb and, forced to stop, glanced at the car beside hers facing in the opposite direction.

'I think you might find it a bit tricky getting a car that size around the corner at the top of this hill. It almost doubles back on itself,' she called to the other driver, now only an arm's length from her.

A pair of eyes as dark as a gypsy's looked back. But there was nothing else gypsy-like in the appearance of the man now framed in the open window of the silver-grey Mercedes so close to her little red hatchback.

A crisp white shirt, the collar outlining the tanned column of his throat, showed off the equally tanned face to advantage. Two well-manicured hands gripped the steering-wheel and a flash of gold came from the paper-thin watch on his left wrist.

There was a barely perceptible shrug from broad shoulders. 'I think I can navigate my car around any sharp corner that this Cornish village has to offer. But——'he nodded and smiled with a flash of white, even teeth '—thank you anyway for the advice.'

His condescension reached across to Dempsey along with, she had to admit, an aura of magnetic sex appeal that made her pulses quicken, even as she frowned her annoyance.

'Suit yourself,' she muttered under her breath, but hoping that her expression would convey something of how she felt.

'Good hunting,' the driver called as the cars inched past one another.

What on earth does he mean, 'good hunting'? puzzled Dempsey as she drove along Fore Street, cutting in by a rank of granite cottages and on to a lane where the hedgerows were dusted with a lacy trim of cow parsley.

She tugged off her hat and shook her hair free as the summer breeze drifted in through the open window, then suddenly realised the point of the man's remark. Her district nurse's hat, a cheeky trilby that she'd inherited from her aunt, who had been the district nurse in the area, before Dempsey took over. The hat, very much like those worn with hunting pink, was so much a part of her that she forgot she was wearing it a times; but it proclaimed her identity to the people of Penmawtha more than her navy blue dress or her hospital training badge ever did.

She drove up to Bal Cottage and the first of her three remaining calls before she went off duty for the evening.

'Are you going to the meeting tonight?' Old Mrs Bagstock winced as Dempsey spoke while putting the last touches to the dressing around the leg ulcer. Dempsey glanced up fondly at the old lady, her hazel eyes smiling an apology, for she realised how sore the leg was. Mrs Bagstock was one of her favourite patients.

'You never complain, do you?' she said.

'No point, my dear. What can't be cured must be endured,' the old lady muttered, biting her bottom lip.

'Well, I hope that doesn't always apply,' Dempsey laughed. 'It wouldn't say much for my job, now would it?'

'I didn't mean that, you silly girl.' Mrs Bagstock leaned forward and carefully rolled her stocking back up over her leg and pulled her skirt straight as Dempsey packed away the spare dressings before going to the old-fashioned stone sink to wash her hands.

'Don't you get a bit fed up on your own?' Dempsey had asked the question many times, and knew what the answer would be. The cottage had been Mrs Bagstock's home all her married life and was now her refuge in her widowhood.

Though picturesque, it was very damp, always with an earthy, mushroomy smell about it, and Dempsey was sure that it contributed to Mrs Bagstock's ill-health. But what could she do? There was no way that anyone could or should try to persuade the old lady to leave her home.

'They'll have to carry me out of here feet first, when the time comes. Till then I don't want for much,' Mrs Bagstock said, reading Dempsey's thoughts.

'How does it feel?' Dempsey pointed towards the newly bandaged leg.

'Much more comfortable.' Mrs Bagstock

wriggled her foot before tucking it into a well-worn carpet slipper. 'You seem to have the touch, Sister. I dread your day off; no one has the knack with my bandage the way you do.' She stretched out a liver-spotted hand and squeezed Dempsey's small square one.

'What was I saying just now?' Dempsey leaned one hip against the edge of the kitchen table and slowly dried her hands on a white huckaback towel. 'Oh, yes. Are you going to the meeting tonight?'

'Yes, I am, and I expect the whole of Penmawtha will be there, don't you?'

'Well, I certainly will be.' Dempsey folded the towel and hung it over a wooden clothes-horse, then picked up her bag and made her way to the door.

'How are you getting there?'

'Jack Penrose is taking me. By the way, there was a very superior visitor in Fore Street today.' Dempsey knew how Mrs Bagstock enjoyed her snippets of gossip. 'He was in this huge car, intending to cut up by Foggy Corner.' She paused, then added with a grin, 'Hope he got stuck.'

'That's not very Christian of you, m'dear. Who was he?'

'I've no idea. He didn't look like our usual summer visitor. And I didn't mean to sound nasty. It's just that he was so off hand when I tried to tell him how tricky the corner is, especially for a car as long as a double-decker bus. Anyway, I must dash. I'll see you tonight. And Mr John Saville,' Dempsey added, nodding her head. 'He's in for a nasty surprise, I reckon. I don't know how he has the nerve; he has nothing to do with this place and then thinks he can come and buy up half the village!' Dempsey snorted.

'Try not to put too much weight on that bad leg, will you?' she called as she shut the ill-fitting back door behind her and walked carefully along the narrow tiled path to where her car was parked.

She stopped for a moment before getting in and took a deep breath as she gazed out over the sweep of farmland and the valley that cut down to a blue mist of sea in the distance. How she loved this bit of country! Everywhere seemed to call out to her. A blackbird trilled joyfully in the middle of a hawthorn bush to her left, accompanied by the echo of a meadow lark from the impossibly blue sky. Beech trees at the far side of the field were already dressed in their brilliant summer green, and even the outline of the tumbledown wheel-house of Cresswell mine fitted in with the scene which she knew and loved so well.

'We'll fight him all we have to,' she muttered, her normally generous mouth narrowed in determination. 'There's no way he's going to build a leisure park on our piece of coastline.'

She knew she was probably unreasonable in the strength of her feeling, but the threat to the place she loved made her feel sick. Even her training in London, much as she enjoyed some parts of the hectic life there, seemed to be an exile, an interval that she had to get through before living her real life. With a shrug, she opened the door of her car, threw her bag on to the back seat and climbed in ready to drive to her other two calls.

One patient was an elderly diabetic who refused to follow his diet, the other call was to check on the progress of an eight-year-old boy who had recently developed asthma. Dempsey hummed to herself as she drove along the narrow road, and her earlier bad mood melted in the warmth of the June afternoon. She passed the end of Fore Street and went into the courtyard at the front of the old people's flats where Mr Tregarron lived.

Her last two visits speedily dealt with, she continued up the steep, winding road that led to the cliff-top, the sea air blowing into the car window and ruffling her mid-brown hair which she modestly called mouse. But in the sun's present light it shone with gleaming coppery highlights, the tendrils curving gently around her pleasant face with its dusting of freckles that Dempsey hated so much, but which, if she did but know it, made her look much younger than her twenty-five years. Parking beside the small holiday flat she was renting at the present time, she clambered from the car, picked up her medical bag from the back seat and hurried indoors.

She had only lived here for two months, since her cottage had suffered a damaged roof in one of the sweeping storms that came in from the Atlantic, but already she had made a considerable difference to the look of the interior with her pictures, cushions and a Bokhara rug in glorious shades of deep red that she had inherited from her aunt.

Putting her bag on the floor beside a highly polished desk that was also a legacy, she quickly entered the details of her calls in her report book, flicked on the answering machine, which was blissfully silent, and shrugged off her uniform as she went into the bedroom.

'Decisions, decisions,' she muttered to herself as she riffled through the garments on the rail in her wardrobe, crunching an apple between white teeth, in lieu of the supper that she hadn't time for now.

Her appearance for this evening was all-important. Should she appear super-efficient, dark grey suit, white blouse and plain court shoes? Should she trade on her femininity, with a full-skirted cotton dress in vivid swirls of orange and tan? After all, she was likely to be called upon to speak at the meeting when the proposals for the amusement park were to be discussed by every-one interested in its possible development.

Pushing her hand through her hair, Dempsey eventually picked out a severely styled dress in soft apple-green, deceptively cut so that it clung to her slim figure, showing it to advantage. Showered and wearing the dress, with matching sandals and a white and green scarf, she was satisfied with her reflection in the mirror before she went out through the front door and got into the car.

Her eyes sparkled in keen anticipation of the battle to come, and before long she pulled up outside the hall where already there were many faces that she knew, people standing in groups as they enjoyed the soft evening air before going inside.

'Looks like a good turn-out, Dempsey,' called Mrs Bagstock as Dempsey walked towards the main entrance, and she smiled and nodded in answer. The hall, built of granite during the time when tin-mining played an important part in village life, reflected the last of the sun in its serpentine patterns. It filled rapidly, and, feeling nervous now, Dempsey pushed her way to the front and on to the small platform.

'Nice to see you, my dear, and looking as pretty as a picture as usual.' Peter Fenton, their vicar, who also looked after two other small parishes, was taking his duties as chairman of the meeting very seriously, making sure the water-jug was full, stacking forms and plans in a tidy pile, then placing the shabby wooden chairs in line as he waited for the other speakers to arrive.

He pushed his glasses on to the bridge of his nose, then glanced along the length of the hall, as the chattering crowd, the women in gaily coloured summer dresses, the men mostly in shirt-sleeves, slowly drifted in and settled themselves in the rows of chairs.

'What time is Mr Saville coming?' Dempsey whispered. Mr Fenton fussed again with the table, then looked at his watch and shook his head.

'He should be here by now. Eight o'clock, the meeting is called for, and it's already ten to the hour.'

'Hello, Sister.' The speaker, a ruddy-faced man, dressed, despite the heat, in a tweed jacket and corduroy trousers, clambered up on to the side of the platform and sank back thankfully on a chair to Dempsey's left.

'Pretty warm evening it's going to be, with all this lot.' Ted Nancarrow, a member of the local council and one of the busiest fishermen on their coast, pulled a snowy white handkerchief from his pocket and wiped his face.

'You're looking well.' He turned towards Dempsey and smiled, but at that moment there was a pause in the buzz of conversation from the hall and Dempsey looked to the rear to see two men walk with long strides past the assembled crowd. At first sight, they could have been taken for brothers, both over six feet, both with dark hair brushed back in similar style. But then, as they climbed up on to the platform, Dempsey saw that the one in front was older, his face heavily lined, streaks of grey in the thick dark hair. The second she recognised immediately, though he was dressed more formally now than when she had last seen him, in a pale grey lightweight suit.

'Dempsey this is Mr John Saville.' Peter Fenton fussed with the introductions. 'And this is his son, Dr Bart Saville.'

'Miss Dempsey and I have already met.' Dr Saville's handshake was firm and decisive, as was his father's.

'Actually, it's Dempsey Prowse, not Miss Dempsey,' she hissed as Mr Fenton tapped on the table-top and called the meeting to order.

'That's a shame,' he whispered back. 'Made you sound like real southern belle!' He drawled the words, then grinned as Dempsey tried to control a blush that stained her cheeks.

Ostentatiously, she looked towards the vicar and tried to concentrate on his opening words. But she was aware that Dr Saville glanced in her direction at intervals, and she wished she'd been sitting at the other end of the platform, rather than so close to him that she could catch the drift of lemon-scented aftershave, and another essence, difficult to define, that was essentially him.

Acutely conscious of his every move, she looked down at the floor, trying not to show how her eyes were drawn in his direction. Barely listening to Peter Fenton's opening remarks, she studied her notes, mouthing the words quietly to herself, trying one or two phrases in her mind.

It was with a sense of shock that she glanced up and saw that John Saville was addressing the audience. He spoke fluently, in a deep rich voice, with just a trace of a northern origin in the inflexions of some of the words.

'I realise,' he said, 'that many if not all of you in this hall tonight are families that have spent your lives in the village and some are likely to be wary of any change that might come about, paticularly from foreigners across the Tamar.' He smiled, and there were one or two polite titters from some of the faces in the front row.

'I'm not asking you to accept the plans out of hand, but please look at the scale model, which will be on show, study the plans at your leisure, and, I promise you, every attention will be paid to the wishes of the local people before anything is definitely decided.'

As John Saville sat down, there were a few desultory claps, then an embarrassed silence for a moment, before Peter Fenton jumped to his feet.

'Are there any questions?' He pushed his glasses more firmly on to his nose, his thinning hair standing on end, and gazed intently at the audience.

'If there's going to be lots of building—and judging by the description of what's to happen, there's bound to be—will local labour be used, or will men be brought in from outside?' Jack Penrose, who farmed at the head of the valley, frowned at the group on the platform. Mr Saville stood again.

'Of course, some of the workforce will have to come with us. But I'm sure you are all aware that things have been difficult with regard to employment here lately. It's not an ideal holiday site——'

Why do you want your park here, then?' a truculent voice form the back of the hall cut in.

'I mean no offence, but there isn't a lot to attract visitors at present, and since the difficulties with the fishing——'

'There'd be no difficulty with the fishing if we were allowed to run thing our own way.' Ted Nancarrow growled the words.

'I realise that, Mr Nancarrow. No one is criticising the local fishing industry, but I think you all must agree that the young people are leaving in quite large numbers because there isn't enough work for them.'

'So now your development is meant as philanthropy, is it?' Jack Penrose was in fine form, thought Dempsey, mentally applauding his words.

'I think we'd better get on to other matters,' Peter Fenton said hastily as a hubbub of voices started at the back of the hall.

'Just a minute, Vicar.' It was Jack Penrose again. 'How about the profit from this here venture? Are local people going to benefit from that?'

'Dr Saville is going to tell us——' Mr Fenton began, but Dr Saville jumped to his feet and cut in quickly.

'We'll be delighted if any of you are interested enough to buy shares in the company. We would feel we were getting your blessing.'

'Better ask the vicar for a blessing,' another farmer called, whose name Dempsey didn't know. 'We've managed here very well for hundreds of years, and if we need any fancy projects we'll see to 'em ourselves.'

There was an angry rumble of agreement from the hall, with fists raised in some sections.

'Order! Order!' Peter Fenton banged the table with his gavel and gradually the voices subsided. 'We will continue by asking Dr Saville to describe what sort of medical facilities will be available if the development goes ahead.' He turned and gestured towards the younger man, who was waiting with barely concealed impatience to begin speaking again.

He stood, tall and relaxed, his suit sitting smoothly on his shoulders, but all the while Dempsey was reminded of a jungle cat waiting to spring. This man could be dangerous if he doesn't get his own way, she thought, listening carefully to what he had to say.

'Good evening, again. I expect you may think it a little odd that a doctor should be concerned with big business, but I am a member of the family firm and its interests are mine.'

Dempsey doodled on her notepad, then turned to look back at the man standing at the edge of the platform.

'I only help my father in a very part-time way; my medicine comes first. But I hope to explain some other implications when—or should I say if,' he corrected, 'if we are able to build the amusement amenities as we hope to.'

When. The word echoed in Dempsey's mind. So he's quite confident that they'll be successful.

'Dr Saville.' She jumped up as he paused. 'If you are proposing to have large areas under construction in the locality, could you give us an idea of what the medical and nursing facilities will be? As the community nurse here, I should tell you that there's a severe shortage of trained staff already, and that's only to provide cover for the residents, and the few summer visitors that we have each year.'

He swung on his heel and looked hard at her and, though her hands were shaking with nerves, bravely Dempsey returned his stare.

'We have no intention of stretching an overstretched service. Of course, there would be proper clinics, possibly an extra GP, certainly more nursing staff.'

'You have a direct line to the Ministry of Health, do you?' As she spoke, she knew how sarcastic she sounded, but the easy manner and confidence of the speaker worried her. In the main body of the hall there were now several heads nodding in agreement with what he was saying.

'Miss Dempsey,' he drawled her name as she had done earlier, 'we haven't all the finer details worked out as yet, but I can promise you your patients will definitely not be made to suffer, and neither would we expect you to increase your workload to beyond its present limits.'

'I wasn't concerned only about my work.' Biting her lip, Dempsey sat down hurriedly, feeling very much at a disadvantage as Bart Saville faced the audience once more and smiled encouragingly.

'I know that not everyone who was going to speak has done so, but as its such a warm evening I think it would be pleasanter if those who wanted to question us about the proposed development could come along to your local public house—the Fishing Smack, I think it's called. The drinks are on us, of course,' he laughed, his face creasing attractively, 'but it will be more comfortable to discuss matters there.'

'Crafty devil,' muttered Dempsey, then grinned an apology towards the vicar as he turned and frowned at her.

'I'll get away, if you don't mind.' She leaned

across and whispered the words, but Dr Saville heard and took her by the arm.

'Haven't you got any questions for me? I'm disappointed—I enjoy a good fight.'

'I've other things to do, so I must decline your invitation, thank you.' Coolly, she shook her arm free and he stepped down from the platform.

'I'll look forward to another meeting. Where are you off to now, if you don't mind my asking?'

'I've a patient to settle for the night, so if you'll excuse me. . .' Dempsey sighed an exaggerated sigh.

'Do you mind if I come with you?' he asked.

'What about your discussions?' Dempsey couldn't hide her surprise, and paused uncertainly.

'I'm sure my father can cope very well, and I haven't seen much of care in the district. Please may I come? I won't get in your way.' He stared up at her, his eyes appealing, and, in spite of herself, Dempsey couldn't prevent a shy smile.

'You should do that more often. You have a lovely smile.' Before she knew what was happening, he put up his arms and swung her lightly to the ground beside him. 'Mm, yes, definitely a lovely smile.'

Dempsey froze, looking everywhere but at him and those amazing eyes, but in her imagination she could still see the thick dark lashes, irises the colour of deepest sherry and the cleft alongside his mouth that was very nearly a dimple and added an unexpected vulnerability to his face. She swallowed nervously.

How could she say what was in her mind without sounding insufferably rude? If she took this man on her visits, not only would her patients, most of whom she counted as friends, think she'd gone over to the opposition, but she would feel herself to be a traitor as well. On the other hand, Philip would enjoy a visitor, no matter who it might be, and he was her only definite call for the evening.

'I have only one call to make, but if you'd like to come along for that I'm sure Philip won't mind.'

'Thanks, Sister. I'll just tell my father I'll be missing for a while.'

'Do you have to report to your father about every absence?'

He didn't reply in words, merely looked at her hard, and as soon as she'd spoken Dempsey regretted saying such a thing. If ever she'd met anyone who was completely his own man, it was Dr Bart Saville.

Moving away down the hall, she couldn't control a flutter of excitement at the thought of spending more time in his company, and she was acutely aware of him following in her footsteps as she went outside into the cooler air, calling 'goodnight' to the many people she knew.

A nearly full moon fought with the last rays of the setting sun, the contrasting light throwing strong shadows by the hall and dappling the edges of a copse of alder trees at the far side of the parked cars. Not speaking, Dr Saville took her arm and led her in that direction.

'We'd better take my car. It's a very narrow road up to Philip's bungalow,' Dempsey said abruptly.

'You don't mean to say that it's more difficult than Foggy Corner? What a wonderful name. Is it usually foggy there? Is that how it came about?'

'No, it's more interesting than that. It's a corruption of "fogous", the name given to subterranean galleries roofed in stone. There are remains of several tin mines in this area.' She paused. 'Oops, sorry about the geology lecture.'

'Not at all; it's fascinating,' Bart Saville said politely.

Dempsey, now wary at the thought of driving this sophisticated man in her cluttered car, stood for a moment as she opened the door and stared across at him waiting on the passenger side.

'I hope you're not one of those people who can't bear to be driven, Dr Saville,' she said firmly. 'I spend a lot of time in my car and know the area well, so I can't stand back-seat drivers.'

'I promise not to say a word. And the name is Bart.' In the half-light, Dempsey could see a cheeky grin cross his face, and she got into the driver's seat and slammed the door, wondering if perhaps she'd bitten off more than she could chew. Hastily scrambling a heap of papers and sample dressings up together from the front seat, she threw them into the back and opened the door for her passenger.

'What's the matter with your patient?' Bart settled himself comfortably and fastened the seat-belt as Dempsey started the engine and gradually pulled away, turning in a tight half-circle to reach the far side of the car park.

They set off down a winding road that took them along a part of the coast where the moon-light dappled the tops of the waves, sprinkling the sea with diamond drops that sparkled and moved in ever-changing patterns. Wheeling gulls mewed overhead as they searched for resting-places to spend the approaching night. Soon the road climbed in a series of zig-zags towards their destination.

'Philip is a paraplegic. He's twenty-two years old, and fractured his lumbar spine when a tractor toppled on to him on his father's farm,' Dempsey explained.

'Twenty-two!' Bart whistled softly through his teeth. 'That's terrible! He definitely severed his spinal cord, then?'

'I'm afraid so, and obviously it isn't easy for him. Luckily his family were able to adapt one of the farm buildings into a bungalow, and it's fitted in such a way that he can be fairly independent.'

Dempsey changed gear and swung the car through a series of bends, turning sharply to where a gabled roof was just visible through the trees, which, bent by the prevailing wind, looked like a row of stooping elderly ladies.

'Philip's house is just down here.' She braked. 'I usually call in at some time during the evening, though his mother sees to most of his needs. And he does an awful lot for himself.'

Bart followed, not speaking, as Dempsey pushed open the door of the little bungalow, where lights from the windows facing on to the drive shone with a cheery glow.

'Hi, Phil, it's me,' Dempsey called. 'I hope you don't mind—I've brought a visitor.' They went through a tiny hall, into a large, open-plan living area with an arched doorway leading into a bedroom.

'This is Dr Saville. Dr Saville, this is Philip Anstey; I was telling you about him.'

The pale young man in the chair spun the wheels and turned to face them, a smile lighting up his dark grey eyes and thin features.

'I hope you don't mind my butting in like this?' Bart stretched out his hand.

'Any friend of Dempsey's is a friend of mine. I'm always pleased to see visitors. It can be quite a long day.' The words, quietly spoken with just a trace of a Cornish accent, were without self-pity, just a statement of fact, as Philip shook hands with Bart. 'Would you like some coffee?'

'No, thank you——' Dempsey began.

'Yes, please,' Bart interrupted. 'I could do with something to wet my throat after the heat in the hall tonight.'

'You were at the meeting, were you?' Expertly, Philip pushed himself into a kitchen area, where all the fittings were at his level, filled the kettle and plugged it in.

'Dr Saville is part of the consortium which is hoping to build,' Dempsey said drily. She donned a plastic apron, then laid out towel and soap, put two sleeping-tablets into a medicine glass on the bedside table in the small bedroom, and filled a water-jug.

'What do you think of the idea of a development?' Bart sat in a small armchair and took the mug of coffee as Philip passed it across.

'I'm not too sure. It would be good to have more employment, that I do know. Unless you're farming or fishing, there's not much to do, and even those two things are beginning to fail.'

There was a flush of excitement on his face as he turned and chatted to Bart, but Dempsey saw how animated his expression was and thought the possibility of a poor night's sleep, which seemed likely with the excitement of a visitor, would be a small price to pay for the interest it aroused.

'I'll help myself to more milk, if you don't mind.' She topped up her mug and sipped her coffee slowly, content to listen to the two men.

At first she found the contrast between Bart's obvious fitness and Philip's weakness painful to see, but gradually Bart's attitude and gentle questioning had Philip talking nineteen to the dozen, and soon she was adding just an occasional comment, content to see the happiness their company was giving Philip.

CHAPTER TWO

'HEAVENS, look at the time!' Horrified, Dempsey held out her arm in Philip's direction and pointed to the hands on her watch. 'Nearly eleven o'clock.'

'Is that bad?' Bart asked, looking puzzled.

'Of course it is. I have to start work tomorrow at eight, and I need my beauty sleep, even if you two are prepared to talk all night.'

Her plastic apron rustling, Dempsey pushed the wheelchair to the bathroom, so that Philip could reach the washbasin, then hurried to the bedroom and folded the duvet tidily, ready to settle her patient for the night.

'Where's Mum this evening, Philip?' she called, aware all the time of Bart's gaze upon her as she went through the nightly routine, and made self-conscious by his stare.

'She and Dad have gone to the meeting. They're late, aren't they?'

'There was a fiendish plot to win over the opposition by inviting them to the Fishing Smack before going home,' Dempsey said drily. 'They're probably there now, and, like us, haven't noticed the time.'

'Hardly a plot, just a bit of simple hospitality,' protested Bart, his smile belying the abruptness in his voice. A soft swooshing sound from the wheels of his chair warned of Philip's approach as he came from the bathroom, his face glowing like a well-scrubbed schoolboy's, bringing with him a fresh clean smell of toothpaste and soap.

'Let me help.' Bart uncoiled himself from his seat, but before he could get to the wheelchair there was the sound of a key in the front door and hurrying footsteps.

'Sorry, my boy.' A middle-aged woman, with the same dark grey eyes as Philip's, her face flushed with anxiety, paused as she came to the door of the living-room and saw that Philip wasn't alone.

'Oh, I wouldn't have rushed quite so much if I'd known Sister was here with you. And. . .' She stopped in mid-sentence and pulled at the top of the flowered two-piece she was wearing as she looked enquiringly at Bart.

'Mrs Anstey, I'm sorry that we kept Philip chatting this late, but I'm just helping him to get ready for bed now. We were so busy talking, we didn't notice the time. Oh, this is Dr Saville.' Dempsey gestured in Bart's direction.

'Mm, yes, I believe I saw you earlier, didn't I? I'm very grateful that you took the time to visit Philip, but now I think we'd better get on.'

'Mum, Dempsey's giving me a hand,' Philip muttered impatiently.

'And so am I,' Mrs Anstey said firmly.

'Oh, all right.' Philip's tone was sulky. 'Anyway, how did the meeting go?'

'I'll tell you about it in the morning. Now off to bed with you.' Hastily she seized the handle from Bart's grasp and went into the bedroom.

'Let me help.' Quickly Dempsey followed mother and son and, with a few deft movements, had the chair positioned alongside the bed. 'Now, where's your plank?' She picked up a short, flat length of wood, which she slotted under Philip's cushion, leaving the other end jutting over the bed. Taking away the supporting arm from the side of his chair, Philip wriggled himself along the temporary seat, then, his face glistening with effort, sank back on to the pillows.

'That was nicely done, Philip. Here's your hoist. Have you got eveything you want?' Dempsey bustled round the bed as she and Mrs Anstey straightened the covers.

'Yes, I'm fine. Thanks for visiting, and thank Dr Saville for me as well. I've thoroughly enjoyed this evening.'

Mrs Anstey still looked strained, but her high colour had faded and, with a grateful smile at Dempsey, she switched on the intercom that connected through to the Anstey farmhouse and kissed her son on the forehead.

'Anything worth watching on the television tonight? Here's your remote control, just in case.'

'Goodnight, Philip.' Dempsey blew a kiss from the doorway.

'Goodnight, Dempsey, see you tomorrow.'

'Big treat tomorrow, Philip,' Dempsey called as she and Bart started to leave. 'Tuesday, physio day.' She laughed at the expression of disgust on Philip's face, then threw her apron into the wastebin, wiped down the surfaces in the kitchen and went outside with Mrs Anstey, a very quiet Bart holding the door open for them both.

They bade Philip's mother a quick goodnight, then walked swiftly to the car.

'Where can I drop you?' Dempsey turned in her seat and gazed in the dim light at her passenger, but for a moment he didn't reply.

'Bart?'

'Oh, sorry. I was just thinking about Philip there.' He shivered. 'I don't know how he copes and remains so cheerful, knowing that he'll never walk again. Are you sure about the spinal cord?'

'No doubt at all, I'm afraid.' Dempsey stared in surprise. If anyone had asked her, she would have thought Bart Saville the last person to be so upset. The contrast between the dynamic, hard-hitting businessman at the meeting and this obviously tender-hearted person was too great for her to take in.

'Of course,' Bart continued softly, 'he's in love with you.'

'What rubbish,' Dempsey spluttered.

'Don't tell me that the thought has never crossed your mind?'

'He's just a boy.'

'Hardly younger than you are, surely.'

'Three years younger, and that's a lifetime in the present circumstances. Philip is my patient and, I hope, a friend. There's nothing more than that in our relationship.' Unconsciously her tone sharpened.

'I'm sorry, Dempsey, I didn't mean to imply. . .' Bart paused, then leaned across and kissed her gently on the cheek. 'I wouldn't do anything to upset you,' he said quietly.

Except encourage your father to build some monstrosity in my beautiful piece of Cornwall, she thought, biting back the words with difficulty.

'Dr Saville, much as I enjoy your company, I must get home, so please, where are you staying?' Absently she touched her cheek, trailing her fingers aross the imprint of his lips, wondering why such a gentle caress should scorch her skin so.

'Sorry. Of course.' He sat upright and stared through the windscreen, his face a blur of whiteness in the silvery moonlight. 'My father will have gone back to our hotel some time ago. If you could drop me off at the Fishing Smack, I'll put up there for the night. It's not too far out of your way, is it?'

'No, but we'd better hurry. If you haven't booked, they could well have shut up for the night.' Quickly reversing the car on to the road, Dempsey shot off in the direction of the village and the public house which stood on the headland overlooking the sea. But her fears were well founded, for when they arrived after a hectic drive, that at times had Bart clinging to the edge of his seat, all the lights were out and it could have been a film set, entitled *The Deserted Village*.

'Oh, blast it!' Dempsey bit her lip and turned to her passenger. 'What do we do now?'

'Sorry, Dempsey. Perhaps we could knock up the landlord.' Dempsey had a sneaking suspicion that Bart was not as upset by the situation as she was.

'Come on, you'd better come home with me. It'll mean sleeping on the settee, but it's quite comfortable with a sleeping-bag.' She sighed wearily and turned the car once more.

'I don't want to cause you any bother, Dempsey. Let me ring my father and get him to fetch me.'

'Don't be silly. By the time he gets here, it'll be morning, and I'll never wake up in time for duty.'

Almost tutting as she drove, Dempsey soon pulled up outside her flat and parked the car with a squeal of brakes, flustered by the way the evening was developing but not sure why.

Once inside, the enforced intimacy of the flat had her so on edge that she became more and more silent, scarcely daring to say anything in case it should be misunderstood.

Don't be so vain, she told her reflection as she scrubbed her teeth and creamed away the remains of her make-up, staring at the bathroom mirror as though at a stranger. Her hazel eyes stared back at her, as large as saucers. Bart hasn't done anything to make you suppose that he feels more than just a casual friendliness towards you, so don't start thinking all sorts of romantic rubbish, she snorted. Just because he gave you a peck on the cheek earlier.

'Bathroom's free,' she called briskly as she stepped into the sitting-room, where she had already arranged the sleeping-bag and a spare pillow on the settee.

'Thanks.' As Bart stood up in his slow, sinuous way, Dempsey's breath caught in her throat. He had stripped off his jacket, tie and shirt, and she stopped for a moment, lost in admiration at the breadth of his shoulders, the deep chest that tapered to trim waist and hips.

'Dempsey, you're staring.' He smiled, a lazy smile.

'Sorry.' Blushing furiously, she pulled her dressing-gown more closely around her and stood aside as Bart went into the bathroom.

'I have to be away shortly after seven,' she added. 'Is that too early a start for you?'

'Whatever suits you. It's very kind of you to go to all this trouble. I'm a real nuisance, aren't I?' He stepped out from the bathroom, wiping a trace of soap from his face, and, not stopping to answer, Dempsey muttered a hasty goodnight, went into her room and closed the door behind her, leaning back against it for a moment as she tried to control her breathing and slow the rapid beating of her heart.

'Careful,' she told herself firmly. 'Don't forget, he's the enemy.' But her dreams, when she eventually fell asleep, were full of the handsome, dark-eyed face, the surprisingly tender smile that had stirred her interest, despite her efforts to remain aloof.

Their breakfast of coffee and cereal was a hurried and nearly silent affair. Seeing it in the cold light of day, Dempsey worried that her action in inviting Bart to stay might give the impression that she approved of the proposed development. In an effort to stay cool, she knew she sounded offhand and almost rude.

Bart made no comment about her distant manner, politely thanking her for her hospitality and for giving him the opportunity to see a small part of her work. As they set out, the air held an almost pearl-like quality, giving notice of the warm summer day to come, but Dempsey saw nothing of her surroundings. She dropped Bart at the Fishing Smack and drove hurriedly to work, sighing with relief.

However, to her surprise, mixed with the relief, a perverse feeling of disappointment that he hadn't mentioned seeing her again hovered at the back of her mind, and she was frowning heavily as she went into the big old house, once a vicarage, that housed the nurses' clinic and GP's surgery.

'Morning, Dempsey. You look a bit flustered. Overslept, did you?' Rita, part-time receptionist, full-time secretary and the lynchpin of the practice in the view of the nursing and medical staff, looked at Dempsey from behind the desk set at the rear of the waiting-room.

'Very nearly,' Dempsey muttered. 'An unexpected guest. What's on the menu this morning?'

'Not too many calls.' Rita placed her heavily framed glasses on her nose and ran a red-tipped finger down the paper in front of her. 'Dr Morgan has nipped over to see Mrs Bagstock before surgery starts. Apparently she slipped getting out of bed this morning, and when Mrs Penrose went in she found her lying on the floor.'

'Oh, no!' Dempsey put her bag down beside the desk and slipped off her navy blue coat, hanging it on the old-fashioned wooden hall-stand in the corner of the reception area. 'Is she badly hurt?'

'I don't think so. But she wrenched her bad leg, so he thought he'd better make sure there was nothing broken.'

'She'll have to think about giving up the cottage.' Almost absent-mindedly, Dempsey picked up the list of calls and glanced over them, her mind worrying at the problem of the old lady.

'Coffee?' Without waiting for an answer, Rita filled two mugs from a filter jug, and Dempsey took one with a murmer of thanks, sniffing appreciatively before taking a mouthful.

'If you tried to move her from that old cottage, she'd not last a week,' Rita continued with their theme. 'It's the only thing that keeps her going.'

'I know that. But how can she stay on there? She's getting more frail every day.'

'It's a pity her children aren't nearer.' Rita scribbled a few notes on a folder, placed it on the in-tray, and looked up as the door opened and the first patient arrived.

'See you later.' Clutching her mug of coffee in one hand and her bag in the other, Dempsey went through to the tiny room she called an office and sank down in the chair. It had once been a pantry, in the days when the house had been a vicarage, and Dempsey was sure that at times she could smell traces of metal-polish, soap and an occasional whiff of lavender. But, compensating for its size, the window looked out over the garden, a large, sprawling patch of green with shrubs along the far end, and there was a faint mist of blue in the distance, where the sea was just visible.

With an impatient shrug, Dempsey jumped up and pushed up the heavy sash-window, sniffing at the draught of fresh air with just a hint of salt in its many scents. A few deep breaths helped to calm her fidgety nerves, and she sank back on to the chair and picked up the calls already listed in Rita's tidy script.

'When Dr Morgan gets back, could you give me a buzz, please?' Dempsey flicked off the intercom at Rita's noise of assent, and started to underline the most urgent calls. But she found it difficult to concentrate, and after a few moments pulled her bag on to her lap to check that she had enough dressings and syringes for the day's round.

But then she stared in surprise at a plain white envelope inside. Thoughtfully she turned it over and over, searching for a name, but it wasn't addressed, and impulsively she tucked her thumb under the flap and ripped it open. As soon as she started to read she could hear Bart drawling the words in an exaggerated southern accent.

Dear Miss Dempsey, I hope it wasn't an embarrassment for you to have me stay last night. If you can put up with my company again tonight, how about dinner? Yours hopefully, Bart. PS. Could we travel in my car this time, please?

She was amazed at the feeling of happiness that swept through her at the sight of the note, her heart beating so fast that she could hardly catch her breath. Smiling to herself, she rang through to

Rita and asked for the telephone number of the
Fishing Smack.

'Have you got a patient to see?' Rita sounded
puzzled.

'No, it's personal,' Dempsey said shortly. Perhaps Bart wouldn't be at the public house anyway.
As far as she was aware, he and his father weren't
staying there—it had just been a convenient place
to take him that morning. And if he wasn't there,
she had no idea how to contact him. 'Never mind,
Rita; I'll leave it now. Is Dr Morgan back yet?'

'Got in two minutes ago. I was about to call
you, but we had a sudden rush of patients.'

'Thanks, I'll see him now.'

Putting the precious card in the pocket of her
uniform, Dempsey made her way through the
waiting area, nodding a 'good morning' to the
dozen or so people already seated there, and
knocked on the heavy oak door of the surgery.

'Hello, Dempsey. I was about to call you. I
expect Rita told you about Mrs Bagstock, didn't
she? Sit down, sit down.' Dr Morgan pushed a
chair towards Dempsey and perched on the edge
of the big old-fashioned desk, swinging a tweed-
clad leg.

It was difficult to remember a time when she
hadn't known David Morgan, firstly as her doctor
when her aunt had been the district nurse and
now as a colleague and friend. His hair was greyer
these days, the blue eyes more faded in the
weathered face, but his energy and enthusiasm
were still that of a young man, and Dempsey was

eternally grateful that she had someone like him to work with.

'How's Mrs Bagstock?' She straightened her skirt as she sat on the rather uncomfortable chair, conscious suddenly that her dress was getting very shabby. It was time she had some new uniforms, she thought, looking at the faded edges on the hem-line and the way the pocket had frayed.

'I'm rather concerned about her.' Dr Morgan pulled a face, leaning back on the desk to pick out a prescription pad. 'I gave her some paracetamol and codeine mixture. I had some in my bag, and Mrs Penrose will get more at the chemist's when she goes into town. But Mrs Bagstock's leg looks a real mess. She hasn't broken any bones, thank goodness, but I'm afraid all your careful dressings of the last two weeks have been upset.'

'Is her ulcer worse?' Dempsey asked, dismayed.

'I think she must have knocked it on that big old wooden bed of hers; the skin has rubbed away again.'

'What do you want me to put on it?' Hastily, Dempsey felt in her pocket for her notepad, but all she had was the envelope with Bart's invitation. Quickly she turned it over and scribbled the instructions on the back.

'I'll try some vaseline gauze, pad it well and leave it for a couple of days, shall I? That seemed to work last time.'

'Yes. If that's no good, we'll have to think of something else. I tried to persuade her to go to have a check-up in Outpatients, but she won't hear of it. Says there are plenty that need looking at more than her.' Dr Morgan stood up and walked behind the desk as the sound of the telephone cut into their discussion, and he picked it up.

'Yes? Yes, she is. Just a moment.' He passed the receiver to Dempsey. 'It's for you.'

'Thanks.' Unsuspecting, she took it and held it to her ear. 'Hello, Sister Prowse speaking.'

'Well, Miss Dempsey, am I glad I caught you before you hurried off on your round of mercy! What's the answer about tonight? You have seen my note, I take it?'

'Bart?' Dempsey murmured the name uncertainly.

'Who else did you think it would be? I realised you wouldn't have my telephone number, so I thought I'd better ring you.'

Dempsey put her hand over the telephone and raised her eyebrows at Dr Morgan, who was ostentatiously studying some notes on his desk. 'Sorry about this. I'll get it transferred.' She depressed the switch to recall Rita and made the request.

'Certainly.' Rita paused a moment. 'Is it one of our list patients?' she asked, her curiosity almost palpable over the line.

'No, personal—I'm on my way to my office.' Dempsey swung round in the doorway. 'See you later. I'll let you know about Mrs Bagstock.'

'You do that.' Dr Morgan peered at her over half-moon glasses before sounding the buzzer for the first patient to come in. Though he was too polite to ask any questions, Dempsey could sense that his curiosity was very nearly as acute as Rita's.

'I'm sorry, Dr Saville, I haven't time to discuss anything now.' Dempsey sat at her desk, suddenly nervous, her mouth dry, and took refuge in formality, ignoring the small sound of displeasure from the other end of the line.

'Well, I'm sorry to have bothered such a busy person. Perhaps you could let me know when you'll be free and I'll try to fit in a call at a more convenient time.'

'I'll telephone you at lunchtime, if that's all right?' The doodles that she drew on her notepad betrayed her sense of uncertainty about seeing Bart Saville again. But he gave her a number to ring, and she scribbled it down, then replaced the receiver after a hurried goodbye.

In a fluster, she finished packing her bag, taking more syringes from the store cupboard and some extra vials of insulin. If she had time, she would try to show Mr Tregarron how to do his own injection—though so far he had lacked the confidence to attempt it.

If he would only stick to his diet, she thought, as she hurried outside, he wouldn't have to bother with any injections.

'Sister!' Dr Morgan's voice reached Dempsey as she opened her car door and put the bag inside.

'Yes?' she called, hoping her sigh wasn't too obvious. Everything seemed determined to hold up her progress, and she prayed silently that there wasn't another name to add to her list. With

Maggie, their care assistant, away on holiday, she would have to do three bed-baths as well as her usual calls, and two of them were at least five miles out of her way.

'Just to let you know, Dempsey——' Dr Morgan hurried up to her, waving a piece of paper '——Mr Tregarron will be away for the next couple of days, so could you miss him off your list? And I wonder if you could call in and see old Joe Summers? He's complaining about that walking-frame again, and you seem to be the only one who can stop his grumbles.'

'Has Mr Tregarron made arrangements about his insulin while he's away?' she asked.

'I'm not sure. Rita took the message, but I wanted to get something from my car, so I said I'd pass it on.'

He turned away with an encouraging pat on her arm and lifted a brown wrapped paper parcel from the boot of his car.

With a squeal of tyres, Dempsey left the surgery and shot out into the main road, narrowly missing an elderly collie dog from the nearby farm.

'Slow down and calm down,' she told herself firmly, her hands shaking as she braked hastily, pulling her foot back from the accelerator and driving in a very sober fashion to her first call.

Joe Summers lived on the far side of the headland in a pink colour-washed cottage that was a twin of Mrs Bagstock's. But the two patients were as different as chalk from cheese. Whereas Mrs Bagstock made light of her infirmities, obviously irritated with herself at times when she couldn't manage, Joe prolonged every visit from doctor or nurse with a list of querulous worries that tried the patience of everyone in the practice. But this morning, to Dempsey's relief, he was on his best behaviour, agreeing to her suggestion that she take his walking-frame to the occupational health department at their local hospital for adjustment, and happy to accept the heavy stick she offered for the time being.

'You seem a bit flustered this morning, Sister.' He followed her to her car and leaned his elbows on the top bar of the gate, his hands unnaturally large with their swollen joints, his grey collarless shirt ruckled around his neck, making him look like an elderly turkey.

'I got a bit behindhand first thing,' she confessed. 'It was one of those days, nothing straightforward.'

'Well, no use getting in a tizzy. What was it, trouble with your young man?' His tone was innocent, but Dempsey could see the mischievous look he gave her as he took a large handkerchief from his trouser pocket and blew into it noisily.

'I haven't got a young man,' she laughed breathlessly.

'Well, none of my business, of course, but I heard you and the young fellow from the development was seeing something of one another.' He gave a throaty chuckle. 'Hope I haven't spoken out of turn.'

'Where on earth did you hear such rubbish?' Dempsey snapped the words out.

'Hey, don't get huffy with me, miss. I've known

your family since before you were born, and
there's no call to get uppity, just because I'm a bit
unsteady on my pins. I've still got my marbles,
you know.'

'Sorry, Mr Summers.' Dempsey smiled an apology. 'I didn't mean to snap. I really have got out
of bed on the wrong side this morning.'

'Well, as long as you don't go speaking like that
again. There's no call for it.' Grudgingly, Joe
Summers waved his hand as Dempsey clambered
into her car and drove away.

For goodness' sake, she thought, a few hours in
someone's company and he's my 'young man'!
And how on earth did Joe hear about it that
quickly, anyway? Shaking her head in amazement
at the speed of the local bush telegraph, Dempsey
continued on her round, trying hard to put Dr
Bart Saville, the whole of the previous evening
and the muddles that seemed to be following her
out of her mind.

She'd always prided herself on her efficiency,
planning the day's routines carefully, even though
care in the community had a habit of throwing
up unexpected problems however thoroughly
Dempsey prepared herself. Unlike hospital, where
the daily routine was run very much to a strict
timetable, work on the district had to be more
flexible. But this morning the problems were of
her own making.

She drove some miles in the wrong direction,
found at one call that she hadn't the necessary
drugs to inject, and finished the morning round at
least an hour later than she had anticipated, hurry-

ing at last into the clinic, her hair awry, her hat perched on the back of her head. 'Any more calls, Rita?' she asked breathlessly as she went past the receptionist, scarcely pausing to wait for an answer.

'Not so far.' Rita leaned over the reception desk and waved an impatient hand at Dempsey's disappearing back. 'But you've got a visitor. . .' Her voice trailed away. 'I asked him to wait in your office,' she muttered quietly as she put a collection of follow-up forms into envelopes and set them on one side.

'Oh, no!' Dempsey paused in the doorway, her face an expression of dismay as her visitor uncoiled himself from the chair and smiled a greeting.

'Well,' Bart said drily, 'I have had warmer welcomes. Don't tell me this is a bad time for you as well?'

'Dr Saville, I'm really rushed off my feet today. I've a care assistant on holiday, there are several more calls to make and I'm about an hour behind with my schedule.'

'Dempsey, heaven forbid that the care of the district should fall by the wayside just because I have a wish for your company. Shall I injure myself in some way, so that I've a legitimate reason for seeing you?'

He leaned towards her and, instinctively, Dempsey pulled her head back, afraid that he might sense how her feelings were in a turmoil at the sight of him.

'Please, sit down. I'm sorry—I really have had

a terrible morning, mostly my own fault.' Piling the armful of papers she was carrying on the desk, Dempsey took off her hat and threw it to one side as she sat in the chair and looked up at Bart, who loomed over her, his frown gradually changing to an expression of mischief.

'I just want the chance to talk to you, but I'd have more success catching a will-o'-the-wisp! You're the most elusive person I've met.'

'Hardly that,' she laughed breathlessly. 'Just a busy working girl.' Picking up her pen, she scribbled a few notes on the edge of a treatment sheet. Anything rather than meet Bart's eyes, for she was afraid he might read on her face how thrilled and flattered she was that he'd made so much effort to seek her out. Before she could say any more, there was a tap at the door and Rita's face appeared in the gap as it opened.

'Sorry to interrupt, Dempsey. Mrs Bagstock on the phone. What time are you going to do her dressing?'

'Heavens, I forgot all about her!' Dempsey hit her forehead with the flat of her hand. 'Tell her I'm on my way.'

'I can see this is impossible.' Quietly, Bart moved towards the door as Rita gently closed it, her face a big question mark. 'If you are able to come, perhaps we can have dinner at the Fishing Smack, say eight o'clock?'

'Yes, that would be lovely. Now I must run.'

He swung back the door with an extravagant bow and, still flustered, Dempsey picked up her bag and hurried out. She really must concentrate on her work and not be side-tracked. However, her thoughts drifted back once more to her visitor as she left the surgery, a vivid picture of dark eyes, that looked almost black at times, at others a deep brown, strong cheekbones and the husky voice that had the ability to send shivers down her spine when she heard it, and, despite her good intentions, there was a secret little smile on her face as she went out to her car.

CHAPTER THREE

'I KNOW I'm late, and I'm very sorry.' Breathlessly, Dempsey hurried to the bar and put her bag on the edge of the stool, next to where Bart was standing. The rest of her day had continued as it had started, and at one point she had thought it likely she would have to refuse Bart's invitation. Mrs Bagstock's leg was much worse by the time Dempsey arrived at Bal Cottage, and she had to arrange an immediate visit to the outpatients department at their local hospital. There had been no one available to collect the old lady after her appointment, and Dempsey, as well as having to make her afternoon calls, had rushed to take Mrs Bagstock back home.

She had barely arrived at the flat and started a leisurely soak in the bath when Mrs Marston, the mother of a young asthmatic, telephoned.

'I'm sorry to disturb you, Sister.' The caller's anxiety was apparent in her voice, a nervous giggle punctuating her words. 'Ben isn't too happy with this new inhaler. He says it makes his heart go fast. Do you think that's all right?'

Controlling a sigh, Dempsey explained that it could happen with that particular drug and that it was nothing to fret over, hoping she'd managed to reassure Mrs Marston.

'But if you're still not happy in the morning,

bring him to the surgery,' she said. 'Or ring me
back later, if you want.'

'Oh, I'm sure that won't be necessary.'

Leaving a trail of wet footprints as she padded
back to the bathroom, Dempsey found the water
had gone cold, and she finished by having a very
scrappy bath.

The long, careful make-up session she had
planned also had to be forgotten, and it was a
very hasty sweep of mascara and lipstick and a
rapid spray of perfume that she applied before she
left the flat.

'You aren't late.' Courteously, Bart pulled the
stool back for her and helped her on to it. 'What
would you like to drink?'

'Just a tonic water, thanks.' Hot and flustered,
Dempsey fanned her face with her bag.

'One tonic, ice and slice, please, and a Scotch
for me.'

Harry Parr grinned at them both as he poured
their drinks and slid the glasses across the bar.

'That's lovely.' Gratefully, Dempsey rolled the
cool glass across her forehead and, for the first
time, looked directly at Bart.

He smiled back at her. 'You look very spring-
like in that dress.'

'Thank you.' She acknowledged the compliment
with a shy nod, and sipped slowly at the cold
drink. Her sundress, with its halter-neck and the
skirt a circle of blue and green flowers on a white
background, was one of her favourites and always
gave her a feeling of confidence. Gradually she
got her breath back and looked around, trying to

ignore Bart's gaze as he gravely studied her. There were few customers in the bar, most preferring to sit outside on the uneven, hummocky grass that served as a pub garden at the back.

For what seemed forever, Dempsey couldn't find anything to say. Her thoughts ran in all directions, wondering if she'd done the right thing in agreeing to meet Bart. In some ways, it still felt a betrayal and, though she hoped that no one in the village would misunderstand, she kept remembering Joe Summers's remarks earlier in the day about her 'young man', and found it difficult to relax.

She was acutely conscious of Bart standing beside her, his hair newly washed and falling forward in a thick wave of blue-black darkness, his eyes glowing in the light from behind the bar. He was casually dressed in jeans and a crisp open-necked shirt, his skin showing golden against the white material.

'I hope you're hungry.' After a lengthy silence, he picked the menu card from the counter and opened it for Dempsey to study. He leaned forward and mouthed the words quietly. 'I'm disappointed that there aren't any local delicacies—just the usual things one can find anywhere.'

'Have you any stargazy pie, Harry?' Her eyes alight with mischief, Dempsey called the landlord over to them.

''Fraid not, Dempsey.'

'Our visitor wants to try a local delicacy,' she explained.

'Should think he's already doing that with you,

in't he?' The voice came from behind them and, as one, Dempsey and Bart whirled around. Joe Summers lifted his glass in salute, then took a large swallow of beer.

'What exactly do you mean by that?' Like a panther, Bart moved across the bar and stood over the old man. Though he spoke so quietly, Dempsey could barely hear the words; the sense of menace was almost palpable, bringing complete silence to the room.

'Nothing,' shrugged Joe, but his hand was shaking as he put his glass back on the table and wiped his face with a large handkerchief, before calling for another drink.

'If I thought you. . .' Bart began.

'Dr Saville, we've got some very nice home-cooked ham, fresh salad and best Cornish new potatoes. How does that suit you?' Quickly, Harry edged from behind the bar and mopped at Joe's table, neatly putting himself between the two men. 'And there's home-made raspberry tart and clotted cream to follow.'

'Sounds delicious.' Smiling coolly, Bart went back and finished his drink. But Dempsey could see a white line of anger around his mouth and suddenly felt sick at the thought that she might be the cause of the trouble.

'Who's that, one of your local characters?' Bart and Dempsey made their way into the dining area. Despite the polished tables and bright pink napkins, it was still a very traditional pub, the bar worn into grooves by the thousands of glasses that had rested on it and the brass foot-rail as shabby as the rest of the fittings. The beams were full of the characteristic aroma of beer and old wood. The only concessions to modernity were the windows, the original ill-fitting frames replaced by dark wood that sat snugly enough to keep out the winter gales.

But now, on this fine summer evening, the windows stood wide, letting in a draught of cool air that lifted the short flowered curtains and brought in the scent of an early-flowering honeysuckle from the wall outside.

'I hope he didn't upset you.' Bart pulled back a chair and ushered Dempsey into it before taking the one opposite. They were the only occupants of the dining-room, and Dempsey sank back with a sigh of relief, glad to escape the watching eyes of the other customers.

'You didn't have to sound so threatening.' Putting her bag on the floor beside her, she picked up a bread roll and buttered it with swift angry movements. 'He's an old man and didn't realise he was being rude.'

'It's lucky he is old.' Bart stopped. 'Let's forget him, shall we? Tell me more about your—what did you call it? Star something pie?'

'Stargazy pie.' Pushing the thought of the earlier unpleasantness from her mind, Dempsey leant her elbows on the table and looked across.

'And what's that when it's about?'

'It's a pie made of pilchards, and the heads are left on and poke up through the pie case so that they seem to be gazing at the stars.' She giggled as a look of disgust crossed Bart's face, her laughter dying away at his expression. 'What's the matter?' she asked.

'You're very sweet, do you know that? I've just decided that I've chosen well with my dinner companion and I'm sure it's going to turn out to be a good evening.' Leaning forward, he kissed the tip of her nose. 'But I think I might give the pilchards gazing at me a miss, if you don't mind.'

'I don't think it would be pilchard time now, anyway. The season used to run from August to October, or thereabouts. But of course. . .' Dempsey paused as she broke off a piece of crusty roll '. . .nowadays the pilchards have disappeared from this coast, and stargazy pie is more a memory than a feature on our menus. Before the turn of the century, pilchards were caught in their millions around here. There was always a 'huer' to alert the village and direct the crews towards the shoals. He would call out 'hevva, hevva'—that's shoal in Cornish—and everyone in the village would have to take part in the salting and packing as soon as the fish were brought ashore.' Lost in her story, Dempsey didn't notice the look on Bart's face as he watched her tell her tale. She would have been surprised at the tender light in his eyes.

'Well, I don't think this is too bad a replacement, do you?' He leaned back as Harry brought their food to the table. Each plate was covered with thick slices of ham, crisp green salad and tomatoes, and Harry returned with a dish of tiny new potatoes that glistened in a garnish of butter and parsley.

'Mmm,' Dempsey crowed, 'I'm starving!'

'Good. Would you like some wine?'

'Well, perhaps just one glass would be nice.' Not looking up, she picked up her knife and fork and attacked her food with relish. There was silence, and both ate hungrily, Bart as appreciative as Dempsey.

'I expect this is a bit boring for you, isn't it?' She leaned back with a sigh of contentment as she placed her knife and fork at rest on the plate.

'Food doesn't have to be French or covered in rich sauces. I enjoy most things, provided they're good.' He wiped his mouth and put his napkin on the table. 'But I think I might have to rest before the raspberry tart—how about you?'

Dempsey nodded. The food and wine had helped her to relax and she was happy to sit just sipping at her glass as Bart topped it up from the tall green bottle between them.

'What do you usually do with yourself in the evening?' Bart waved a finger in Harry's direction and the landlord brought a bottle of mineral water and set it down.

'Not a lot. I'm quite often on call. I might go for a walk along by the cove at this time of year and I like a swim, but that's usually in the early morning,' Dempsey answered.

'You're not one of those keep-fit fanatics, are you? You make yourself sound a regular Amazon! Though I'm positive Amazons didn't have freckles and tawny eyes.' Bart laughed softly at Dempsey's expression and suddenly leaned forward and took her hand, gently separating the fingers. 'And you live by yourself? You're not married or engaged, then? Don't you ever get lonely?'

'Not really. I keep busy, and there's always something going on in the village.' Though she had to admit to herself, if not to Bart, that recently she had begun to wonder if there weren't more to life than her usual round of visits and clinics.

She laughed at the look of disbelief on his face.

'It's true,' she reiterated. 'It may not seem likely to someone who's used to the flesh-pots of London, but we aren't completely cut off from civilisation, whatever you might have been told.'

'I'm very relieved to hear it. My father has left me in charge here for the time being; he has to go to New York at the weekend, so he went off in the company helicopter this afternoon.'

'How do you manage to fit in business and medicine?' she asked. 'What branch of medicine are you in, by the way?'

'I've been working on a research programme for the past year. A colleague and I have been studying remission in multiple sclerosis and seeing if there's a pattern. You probably know that MS is one of the neurological diseases where there's a loss of the myelin sheath around the actual nerve fibres, and the cause isn't really understood. I'm inclined to believe it might be viral in origin, but we weren't looking at that aspect of it, more trying to find out why there are remissions and if the remissions in the illness could be lengthened.' Bart paused and took a sip of wine.

'I wouldn't have pictured you as working in

research,' Dempsey said, her eyebrows raised in surprise.

'Why not?' Bart's tone was defensive.

'Well, you don't look like a background type to me.'

'What type do I seem?' He spoke softly and stared into her eyes, and Dempsey, flustered, picked up her glass and looked at the wine, studying the bubbles intently.

'You're not married or engaged or anything, then?' she blurted out. And she couldn't explain the feeling of relief as Bart shook his head.

'No commitments. I can assure you, I'm very good in my line of work and I enjoy fighting against the odds, which is what research very often is. Anyway, I hate to think of any young person incapacitated, and multiple sclerosis is, more often than not, an illness of the young.' Again, he took a mouthful of wine, then continued, 'Besides which, I'm very stubborn and don't give up easily on going after what I think is worthwhile.'

Was he warning her in a roundabout way about the development? Or did his words have another deeper meaning? There was something in the way he was looking at her. . .

His voice broke into her thoughts. 'Anyway, I've all our findings to write up, but first I'm having a well-earned rest. Three months off, which has fitted in very well, as it happens.'

'Won't you forget all your results?' asked Dempsey.

'Shall I bring your sweets now?' Harry appeared

at the table, interrupting them, and with a sense of shock Dempsey realised that it was already getting near to closing time. 'My wife would like to get cleaned up in the kitchen,' the landlord continued apologetically.

'Of course. Sorry to have held you up,' Bart apologised. 'I forgot you would keep early hours here.'

'We're not all moribund rustics,' Dempsey said in exasperated tones. 'But I for one will have to get back soon. I'd like to be home by twelve.'

'Just like Cinderella.' Bart took a mouthful of tart and they both said little, concentrating on finishing their meal.

At intervals, when she thought Bart wasn't watching, Dempsey glanced up from under her lashes. She couldn't remember having been in the company of a man who so effortlessly conveyed an aura of almost animal magnetism. When he took her hand, when his fingers brushed hers as he added wine to her glass, when he looked at her teasingly, it was like an electric shock stirring at her senses, and she knew it would be difficult to hide how attracted she felt if she spent much time in his company.

Remember it's war, she told herself sternly, and she straightened in her chair and frowned at him.

'Let me ask you a question,' she said shortly. 'Why did you ask me out?'

'Oh, come, let's not have any false modesty. You're a very pretty girl, I get the impression you're bright and are fun if and when you let your hair down, and I thought I'd like to get to know you better.'

'You sound very condescending at times, did you know that?' The offended expression on Bart's face at her words brought a peal of laugher to Dempsey's lips. 'Sorry,' she spluttered, 'but you looked so shocked at the idea.'

'I don't really sound superior, do I? I don't feel it.'

'Maybe not, but sometimes. . .' she paused '. . .well, I won't say any more.'

'No, you won't. That's enough about me.' Bart pushed his plate away from him and leaned on the table. 'What about your family? Are they living locally?'

'My parents are in Zimbabwe; my father's a training manager in the copper mines there, and, where he goes, my mother's right there with him.' She gave a wry smile. It was difficult to describe her parents' devotion to one another without sounding sentimental. Still, it had helped Dempsey and her brother become very independent, as they'd learned to fend for themselves while their parents travelled the world.

Their aunt, actually a cousin of their father's, had been the mainstay in their young lives, taking care of them; Dempsey couldn't remember a time when she hadn't wanted to be a district nurse like Aunt Jess. Even though it had been two years since her aunt's death, Dempsey missed her sadly, looking in vain for the common sense her aunt had dispensed as well as the care she had lavished on Dempsey and Richard. Now Richard was married and living in Plymouth, and Dempsey realised once again that she was the only one of the family left to defend the village, as it were, that had been part of their life for generations.

'Has your father always been a miner?' Bart's voice broke into her thoughts.

'Afraid so.' Dempsey shivered. 'I don't know how he can bear it, always underground somewhere. Even with this present job, where he's really in administration, I bet he finds plenty of excuses to get to the workface.'

'Well, I suppose he follows a long tradition, being from this area.'

'You can say that again.' Dempsey grinned. 'You know the definition of a mine, don't you?' Bart shook his head. 'It's a hole in the ground with a Cornishman at the bottom.'

'And you've never felt like straying far from home?'

'No, thank you. London was far enough for me when I did my training.' She took a sip from her glass, then looked back across the table. 'What about you? Where's your home?'

'Where do you think?'

'Mmm.' Dempsey pondered and studied the handsome face, noting how Bart sat half turned to the table, an arm draped easily on the back of his chair, fitting in completely, even in a place probably very different from his usual surroundings.

The noise of a moth fluttering against the table-lamp sounded in time with the beating of her heart as he stared back at her with eyes half closed.

'I should think Home Counties, public school, training in one of the big London hospitals,' she said hastily, putting her glass back on the table with a bang.

'Am I that transparent?' Bart gave a rueful laugh. 'Nearly right; my family comes from Yorkshire, but my father moved to the south-east when I was very young, and I've spent most of my life there.'

'And what about your mother?'

There was a silence for a moment. 'My mother couldn't keep up with the pressures of being a rich man's wife and left when I was nine.'

'Oh, I'm sorry,' she said softly.

'There's nothing to be sorry about. It was twenty years ago, after all, and my family isn't the only one to be affected by divorce.'

'And didn't your mother want to take you with her?'

'I don't know, and I really don't care very much.' His eyes were suddenly opaque, the irises as dark as Cornish slate, not showing any trace of emotion; but for a moment there was an impression of hurt under the casual words, and Dempsey felt a rush of sympathy for the small boy that had been Bart.

'Anyway, my father and I have remained very good friends, and there's nothing I wouldn't do for him.' He paused. 'Would you like a brandy or a liqueur?'

'Oh, no, thanks. I must get home. I'm quite

happy with my two glasses of wine, especially having to drive.'

'But I'll get you a taxi, don't be silly.'

'What taxi?' she queried.

'Well, there must be a private hire car available.'

'I'm perfectly all right to drive. Don't forget I know the roads round here really well. I'm out and about on them all the time.'

'Well, if you're sure, I'll get the bill and see you on your way. Don't drive as you did last night, will you?'

'What's that supposed to mean?' Offended, Dempsey shrugged away Bart's supporting arm from her waist as they walked through the bar. She knew she drove fast, but she prided herself on knowing the locality well enough to make her driving almost instinctive.

'Nothing. Don't look so cross.' They reached the main door and Dempsey turned to call, 'Goodnight' to Harry. The bar now was empty, all the other customers gone, and she felt very vulnerable at being alone with Bart as he took her arm once more and they strolled towards her car.

A nearly full moon was hidden in a drift of mist that almost obscured the trees at the edge of the small car park and lent a sense of unreality to the scene. Dempsey thought how romantic the traces of light from the pub windows were, with a shimmering quality that increased the feeling of fantasy. She was completely unprepared for Bart's reaction.

'That's it.' He pulled her to an abrupt halt.

'You're not driving home in fog. You could miss your way, drive off a cliff—anything.'

'Hey, it's only a bit of sea-mist. We get it a lot in the mornings and evenings, with the changes of temperature from the sea.'

'I'm not about to start a discussion on the weather patterns in this God-forsaken spot. That is fog——' Bart gestured towards the road '—and I'm not letting you risk your life driving in it.'

'It is not a God-forsaken spot, and I'm going home in my car, and I really don't think you have the right to say what I should or should not do.' Angrily Dempsey moved away, her earlier impressions of a romantic evening gone in a moment. What a bossy pig, she thought huffily. As though I'm not capable!

'Wait there,' the 'bossy pig' instructed. 'I'll go and see if there's a room free.' Swinging on his heel, Bart went into the bar again, and as he disappeared from view Dempsey ran across to her car and opened the door.

The mist lifted and she was able to see quite clearly as she started the engine and drove swiftly along the coast road and the short distance to her flat. It wasn't only resentment about Bart's high-handed attitude that pushed her on. She was well aware that too much time in his company was undermining her resolve to fight the plans for the development, in a way she hadn't expected, and the safety of the flat called to her like a refuge.

But she wasn't surprised when the telephone rang almost as she walked through the door.

'I suppose you think you're very slick.' The

words seemed to drop into her ear like cubes of ice. 'If I hadn't had several glasses of wine, I should be coming to tell you face to face what I think about devious women.'

'There was nothing devious in what I did. And, as you can hear——' Dempsey couldn't keep the note of triumph from her voice '——I got home safe and sound. Sorry if you were worried.' But she was talking to an empty line, the buzz drowning her words as Bart hung up without saying any more.

'Oh, phooey!' she said to the receiver as she slammed it down. She felt as flat as a collapsed balloon and threw her dress and underwear in an untidy heap before scrambling into bed. 'Damn you, Bart Saville,' she whispered, thumping her pillows into shape. 'I'm not going to let you get under my skin.' But somehow she knew, as she drifted off to sleep, that it would be easier said than done.

CHAPTER FOUR

'THANK goodness you're here, Dempsey.' Rita, her plump face corrugated with worry, waved a welcoming hand in Dempsey's direction and turned to the rear of the reception desk, pulling out a piece of paper, which she thrust under Dempsey's nose. 'Take a look at that. I found the message on my table when I came in this morning.'

Curiously, Dempsey took it, and, after struggling for a moment to decipher Dr Morgan's spider-like writing, read the words.

Dear Rita, Sorry to spring this on you, but I'm sure you will cope in your usual exemplary fashion. I've been called to Cardiff. Jenny's been in a car accident and Mary and I will be nearly there by the time you open up the surgery. Apologise to Dempsey for me that I didn't get in touch, but I've arranged a locum, so no problems on that score. Will ring when we have news. David Morgan.

'Oh, no—poor Dr Morgan! I hope Jenny will be all right. They must be worried to bits—their only daughter.' Dempsey whispered the words to herself as Rita took the short letter and read the message again. 'What's the matter with her; have you heard? And I wonder why he didn't phone one of us?'

'I believe they left at about two o'clock this morning, so, knowing Dr Morgan, he wouldn't want to wake us.' Pensively, Rita tapped her pencil against her strong white teeth.

'Who's the locum; does David mention it anywhere?' Dempsey turned the paper over, but there was nothing more.

'I've got that written down. I reckon it'll cause a bit of a stir in the village—wait till you see the name.' As Rita spoke, Dempsey felt a sudden tightening of her stomach, already knowing what the receptionist's next words were going to be.

'Don't tell me. A certain Dr Saville has stepped into the breach,' Dempsey grimaced.

'Got it in one.' Rita stared curiously. 'I thought you liked him?'

'I've been trying to avoid him for the past week. We seemed to spend a lot of time in one another's company during his first couple of days here, and I thought it wasn't really a good idea.'

'Lucky old you. I wouldn't mind a few days in his company—nor nights, come to that.' Rita giggled suddenly. 'Though I think Frank might find it a bit crowded!'

Dempsey giggled in sympathy. Rita's rather large husband worked on one of the local fishing-boats, and when he wasn't fishing was the anchor man of the village tug-of-war team. Their merriment was interrupted by the noise of the door swinging back, and Dempsey sensed who it was even before she looked around.

'Well,' said the familiar voice, sending prickles down her spine, 'it's a bit surprising to hear all this laughter when Dr Morgan is so worried about his daughter.'

Full of guilt, the two friends were immediately silenced.

'Good morning, Doctor.' Primly, Rita straightened, then picked up a file from the desk, not looking in Dempsey's direction.

'It's nice to have you working with us, Dr Saville.' Taking a deep breath, Dempsey turned and looked up at the face that had haunted her dreams for the past week.

'Good morning, Sister. Rita, perhaps when you have a list of patients for me you'll bring them through to the surgery and we can make a start.' Ignoring Dempsey any further, Bart pushed open the door of the doctor's office and went inside.

'Well!' Rita exclaimed. 'He doesn't sound too happy. I'd better hurry up and take these files to him.'

But Dempsey hardly heard her words. She hurried into her own small room and sat at the desk, not seeing the paperwork awaiting her attention. Why had Bart been so offhand? She realised that they had parted on a slightly sour note, after their meal at the Fishing Smack, but surely there hadn't been enough bad feeling to cause him to look through her the way he had?

The fact that he hadn't made any effort to contact her in the intervening days had in some ways been a relief, for she was frightened at how strongly she was attracted to him. But there wasn't any reason for him to behave as if there had been a major quarrel.

Doodling on a scrap of paper, Dempsey tightened her mouth in sudden determination. She would go and talk to him right now. If they were to work together for some little while, there could be no bad feeling. Quite apart from any personal implication, it could affect everyone. Spraying herself with a drift of flowery cologne and smoothing on extra lipstick, she picked up the files of two patients who were due for calls that day and walked firmly up to the surgery. Rapping sharply with her knuckles and not waiting for an answer, she flung open the door and marched in.

'I would prefer that you wait for me to say "Come in", Sister, and not barge in, in that way. I might have a patient here, and it could be embarrassing.'

'Bart, what on earth's the matter?' Her expression pleading, Dempsey moved towards the desk and stood in front of it. 'I'm sorry if I've done something to offend you. Won't you explain so that I can apologise? If it's because I drove off the other evening. . .' Her words trailed away.

'It's nothing like that.' Suddenly Bart's voice was softer. 'But I think it's not wise for us to become too friendly. People could get the wrong impression, and, as we're such poles apart in our views on the development, it's better if we stay away from one another.'

'I can understand if you don't want to mix with me socially, but you might at least show some courtesy at work.' Horrified at the lump she could feel tightening her throat, Dempsey swung round and ran back to her office. She dashed at the suspicious moisture in her eyes, trumpeted into a tissue, and picked up the list of calls for the day, which Rita, with her usual efficiency, had typed.

'Damn, damn, damn,' she muttered, trying to read the names with eyes that were blurred. Not stopping to analyse why she should be so upset, she packed various dressings in her bag, took the list and walked out into the reception area.

'Are you off already?' Rita looked up in surprise. 'I was about to pour your coffee.'

'I won't stop,' Dempsey said in muffled tones.

'Come on, have some coffee. How can you do your round without your caffeine fix?' Taking her by the arm, Rita ushered her into the reception cubicle and thrust a mug of coffee into her unresisting hand. 'Here, put your bag down, take the weight off your feet and tell me why you've got a face as white and as miserable as a stuck pig.'

'You are an idiot, Rita,' Dempsey grinned shakily. 'I feel better already. It's all to do with Bart.'

'Is that his name? Hmm, suits him somehow.' Matter-of-factly, Rita picked up her mug and took a large gulp as she waited for Dempsey to continue.

'It's nothing; I'm tired and over-reacting.'

'I'm not surprised you're tired. You need a break. Did Ben's mother ring you again last night?'

Dempsey nodded.

'She'll have to learn to cope. Ben's asthma is never going to improve with his mother a constant bundle of anxiety,' Rita said sharply.

'Well, it's understandable, with her being a widow and Ben her only child. I don't mind her ringing me for reassurance.' Dempsey placed her mug on the desk. 'Actually, I'm going to suggest an appointment for him to have some lung-capacity measurements done.'

'Some what?'

'You know—Ben to blow into a type of respirometer and for his lung capacity and resistance to be measured on a vitalograph. I didn't want him to have the tests before because I thought all the paraphernalia in Outpatients might make him nervous, but if it will stop his mother fretting it could be the answer.'

'Is his asthma very bad?'

'Not really. In fact, he has very little bronchospasm and no infection, and the new nebuliser is working very well. With luck, he'll grow out of it, anyway, as he gets older. He's a lovely little chap, quite matter-of-fact about it all; it's Mum who's the problem.' Dempsey paused. 'When Aunt Jess was in training, they used to say that asthma couldn't kill you.'

'And can it?' asked Rita.

'Well, I remember when I was in ITU there was a woman with asthma brought in. She'd arrested in Casualty, they resuscitated her and intubated her. By the time she got to the unit, she arrested again and we had a job to get her heart going. Luckily, those cases are few and far between, but I can't help sympathising with Mrs Marston for getting upset sometimes.'

'She always was a worrier,' said Rita, 'and I don't think you'll change her now.'

'If you don't mind, Rita——' Dempsey looked at her watch '—I'll leave you to cope with our locum and I'll try and finish my calls a bit earlier and give myself a half-day.'

Rita patted her shoulder, but didn't say any more as the buzzer from the surgery sounded impatiently. Picking up a notebook and pencil, she raised her eyebrows at Dempsey and hurried away.

The weather, after early morning mist, had brightened by the time Dempsey went out to her car, the sun dazzling through the windscreen. Putting on her sunglasses, she started the engine and pulled away. Her mind in a turmoil, with thoughts of Bart, worry over David Morgan's daughter, combined to take her concentration from the road, and she suddenly looked round and realised that she had absent-mindedly driven along the coast road and was at the sandy end of the small bay near her cottage.

On impulse, she stopped the car and clambered out, scrambling down a rocky slope to the little curved beach, which, this early in the day, was completely deserted. Kicking off her shoes and delighting in the feel of the sand on her feet, she hitched her uniform dress above her knees and ran like a child down to the water's edge. Its icy temperature made her gasp, and she paused as the first wave washed over her toes, then, taking a deep breath, she waded into the water and strode along the edge of the beach towards the far end.

Gulls wheeled overhead, chorusing impatiently as they swooped and dived, several small crabs scuttled from her path and drifts of seaweed tickled her feet as she paddled through the surf. She sniffed at the fresh tang brought in by the sea breeze, and paused to watch a small coaster on the horizon chug its way towards the Bristol Channel.

If Bart wanted to keep their relationship on a business footing, so be it. No man, however attractive, was worth the risk of spoiling this beautiful coastline and the age-old character of the village, which she loved so well.

Feeling mentally and emotionally refreshed, Dempsey ran back lightly across the sand, waving to an astonished fisherman who had arrived and was sitting on the rocks at the base of the cliff as she climbed up the path to her car.

She pulled out a box of tissues to dry her feet, and didn't notice the car that edged up alongside. The voice through the window made her jump so suddenly that the tissues flew in the air and fell slowly around her like lazy pink snowflakes.

'You could give a girl a heart attack, creeping up on her like that,' she snapped as Bart hastily gathered the stray pieces of paper and bundled them back through the open window.

'I'm sorry, Dempsey, I didn't mean to frighten you. I'm glad I've seen you; I wanted to talk where we wouldn't be interrupted.'

'Haven't you got any calls?' she said sharply,

thinking how difficult it was to seem professional as she sat barefoot, her hair blown over her face and her uniform dress pulled above her knees. 'As you can see, you've caught me at a disadvantage.' She gestured at her bare legs and silently prayed that he hadn't been there as she'd gambolled at the water's edge a few minutes earlier. But her wish wasn't to be granted.

'You looked as though you were having a lot of fun down there on the beach,' he observed.

A slow drift of colour rose in her cheeks and she stared quickly out of the opposite window, her attitude daring him to say any more.

'Can I get in the car with you, or would you prefer to sit in mine?' He straightened.

'I'd better not get in that lovely machine with all this sand on me.' Ungraciously, she opened the passenger door, and Bart moved round behind the car and slid into the seat, looking, as always, completely at ease.

Doesn't he ever get flustered? Dempsey thought grumpily as she struggled into her shoes and waited for him to speak. His manner was relaxed, the cream casual shirt, striped tie and suede jacket fitting perfectly, his lightweight trousers snug on the long and powerful thighs.

'What's the matter?' he queried. 'Aren't I properly dressed for a country GP?'

'You know very well that. . .oh, never mind. What did you want to discuss with me?'

Bart leaned across and took her hand. 'You're still cross about the way I spoke to you this morning, aren't you?'

'Well, you must admit, you were very offhand.' Nervously, Dempsey pulled her hand free and gazed out through the windscreen, anywhere but at Bart. A sharp flurry of breeze stirred at her hair, lifting it from the nape of her neck, and she shivered, then froze as Bart's fingers followed, smoothing her skin.

'Mm, you smell of the sea and fresh air,' he murmured softly.

'Haven't you got some patients to visit?' Dempsey's voice came out in a hurried squeak and she covered her confusion by bending forward and re-tying her shoelace.

'Not actually any to see. I'm lucky that I've had to take over on a Saturday, when there isn't a formal surgery and, as it happens, few calls. Have you any particular problems that you want to discuss?' Stretching in the seat, Bart adopted a businesslike tone, and Dempsey felt a flutter of relief that the moment of intimacy had passed. 'How is Philip, by the way?'

'Well, he doesn't alter much. I'd like to think of an interest for him—the hours must drag terribly. And, despite his physiotherapy, his legs are very wasted. His parents suggested getting him a computer, but I think Philip misses physical activity as much as anything.' Absently, she pulled at a thread in the hem of her dress.

'Are there any other patients that I should be concerned about? Rita filled me in with some details, but I thought there might be other points that you could add.'

'The only one that comes to mind is Ben

Marston; he's an eight-year-old who recently developed asthma, and his mother is a terrible worrier. I thought about doing some vital capacity lung tests—to reassure his mother as much as anything.'

'That's good thinking; can you arrange it or shall I get in touch with the hospital outpatients?'

'I can do it. Now I must get on.' Pulling her skirt straight, Dempsey took hold of the ignition key.

'Just before you do depart——' Bart rested his hand on hers '—I wondered if perhaps we couldn't have a truce over the development.'

'A truce? How do you mean?' Dempsey's hazel eyes narrowed questioningly.

'I thought it might be a good idea for you to show me around Penmawtha, and give me an insight into how village life goes on, then I'll try and tell you why I think the leisure centre is a good idea. Not only for Saville Enterprises but also for the village as well.'

'You seemed to think we ought not to spend too much time in one another's company, when you spoke to me this morning.' Dempsey knew she sounded petulant, but was unable to stop herself. Every time she thought she had the measure of Dr Bart Saville, he disconcerted her in some way. If she were truthful, she couldn't think of anything she would like better than to introduce him to the village, but would it do any good? Not to her heart, a voice deep inside her warned, but she pushed the treacherous thought away and concentrated on what Bart was saying.

'Aren't I allowed to change my mind, or is that woman's prerogative only?' He laughed softly. 'You do get on your high horse about things at times, don't you? You should see your expression.'

'I do not!' Hastily, Dempsey turned the rear-view mirror towards herself, and gasped as she saw the tumbled mass of her red-brown hair and streaks of sand vying with the freckles on her face.

'Oh, God,' she moaned, 'what a mess.' She pushed herself up in her seat and switched on the engine. 'Out, out, out! I'm going to my flat for a wash and brush up, then I'm off to see my patients, leaving the rest of the weekend clear, I hope.' Without waiting for an answer from Bart, she leaned across and flung open the passenger-side door, managing with difficulty to hide the tremor that ran through her as her arm accidentally brushed against his powerful chest.

'I can take a hint.' Laughing, Bart climbed out and leaned down, resting his hand on the top of the still open door. 'I'll pick you up at your flat at about two. Does that give you time to get round your patients?'

Dempsey nodded, and couldn't prevent a mischievous grin as she roared off and saw the look of horror that crossed Bart's face as she did so.

'Two o'clock,' she sang from the open window of the car as she drove the short journey home. What shall I wear? Where shall we go? she wondered. And——her face sobered suddenly as she pulled up and jumped out of the car —I must find out if Rita has heard anything from David. As she opened the front door and ran inside, the telephone was ringing as though in answer to her thoughts, and she managed to reach it before the answering machine cut in.

'Hello? Hello, who's that?' The voice at the other end of the line was muffled for a moment, then David Morgan sounded more clearly.

'Oh, good, Dempsey, I'm glad I've caught you. I tried the surgery, but Rita must have left——'

'How's Jenny?' Dempsey interrupted anxiously.

'She has a spinal injury.'

'Oh, no; how bad?'

'We're not sure yet. I'm hoping to see the neurosurgeons this afternoon, and we might know a bit more. She's had a CAT scan and there's a lesion at her lower thoracic spine, at waist level, but how much damage to the cord, they haven't said.'

'Similar to Philip, then. What do you want me to do?' asked Dempsey. 'Is Mary all right? Do you want anything?'

'What I'm really ringing about is to say that obviously we don't want to leave here at present, so do you think you can cope with the practice?'

'Forget everything here.' Dempsey pulled the telephone cord to its full length and flopped back on to the settee, flinging her legs over the arm. 'Dr Saville seems very efficient, and Rita and I can see to any problem he can't deal with.'

'It is a bit of a funny situation having him, but he was there right on the spot, and was very keen. . . Oh, I'll have to go—money's running out. Bye, Dempsey; I'll ring again.'

The click on the line seemed to echo for a long moment as Dempsey sat, lost in thought, before replacing the receiver. So Bart Saville was very keen to do the locum job. Impatiently she ran her fingers through her hair. Was it just a willingness to help a fellow medic in an emergency, or was he thinking it would be an ideal way to get into the good books of the people of Penmawtha?

She scrambled up from her undignified position and wandered into the bedroom, but had to return as the telephone shrilled out another summons.

'Sister Prowse,' she said, her mind still on the previous call.

'It's Vera Summers, Sister.'

'Who?' Dempsey said sharply.

'Vera Summers, Joe Summers's daughter.' Vera Summers, a mouse of a woman with a voice to match, whispered her name apologetically. 'I'm sorry to bother you, Sister, but I can't get hold of Dr Morgan, and Dad's had a funny turn—looks like a stroke. . .' Her voice trailed off, but Dempsey could hear that her caller was on the verge of tears.

'The doctor has had to go away suddenly. I'll come over right now. Joe hasn't been sick or anything, has he?'

'No, he'd just finished a cup of tea and was in the armchair, reading the paper, when there was a horrible gurgling noise, and now his face is all lop-sided.'

'Just keep him in the chair, if you can; I'll be there in about ten minues.'

Dempsey gathered up her medical bag and

pulled a comb through her hair before hurrying
out. But she ran back indoors again and scribbled
a message on a sheet of paper, which she taped to
the front door before getting in the car and driving
off. Bart might call, and it seemed the easiest way
to let him know where she was.

Vera Summers would be in a terrible state, she
thought, as she pulled out on to the main road
and drove past the edge of the bay to the far
headland and Joe Summer's cottage. Bullied for
most of her life, verbally if not physically, Vera
had been left with little confidence, and if anything happened to Joe she would be completely
lost.

'Cross that bridge when we come to it,'
Dempsey told herself as she drove up the final piece
of road that led to the track and so to the cottage.

She had heard of people wringing their hands,
but she'd never seen it actually done until she
opened the door of the Summers's cottage and
was greeted by an anxious Vera. The other woman
stood by the chair where the old man slumped,
and her hands folded and twisted into a coil.
Dempsey went over to inspect the patient, whose
head hung slackly to one side. His right arm was
flaccid, resting on the corduroy-clad knee, with as
little form in it as a jellyfish.

But he hadn't lost consciousness, and though
his speech was slurred Dempsey was able to make
out the few words that he struggled to say as she
bent over him, took his pulse, then looked at his
pupils, which were typically uneven in size.

'I'm sorry. . .sorry about the. . .' His voice failed.

'Don't worry about trying to speak, Joe,' Dempsey said gently. 'It looks as though we'll have to get you to the hospital for a few tests and things.' She took a tissue and wiped a trickle of saliva from the corner of his mouth.

'Don't want to. . .'

'I'm afraid you'll have to go in for a little while.'

'That's right, Dad, they'll soon sort you out,' said Vera.

'Where's the doctor?' Joe struggled up in the chair, but the effort was too much for him and, with a wheezing breath, he sank back again. 'Got terrible headache,' he muttered, then closed his eyes as though the small amount of light that came through the cottage window was too much to bear.

'Oh, Sister——' Vera quavered.

'Here's what I'd like you to do,' Dempsey interrupted as she took Vera by the arm. Anything to keep her busy, she thought, looking at the middle-aged face that was as crumpled as used tissue paper. 'It would be best if you packed pyjamas, toilet things and anything else you can think of, for your father to take with him, while I organise an ambulance. May I use the phone?'

'We're not on the phone; Dad would never have one. I had to go to the one on the corner of the main road to ring you.'

'No phone?' Dempsey studied her patient. She wasn't very happy at the thought of leaving him and Vera while she went to get an ambulance. His face was badly puckered and she was afraid he might slip from the chair to the floor. But she would be able to explain the situation so much more coherently than Vera. She paused, then, with a hurried pat on her patient's arm, opened the door and stepped outside.

The sight of a silver-grey Mercedes pulling up by the gate was as welcome as could be.

'Bart!' She ran towards him as he stepped from the car and pushed open the gate.

'You dropped this near your car earlier on, and I didn't know if it was important——' he waved a black notebook in the air '—so I went to the flat and saw your note. I would have been here sooner, but I'm not used to finding places without any sort of road name or number.' He looked at her with raised eyebrows as Dempsey seized his arm.

'Have you got a car phone?' she demanded.

'Well, yes.'

Dempsey blew out her cheeks. 'Phew, you're the answer to a maiden's prayer!'

'Well, I've been called a few things in my time,' he laughed. 'What's the problem?'

'Joe Summers has almost certainly had a stroke and there isn't a phone at the cottage. I was just about to go and ring for an ambulance, but I'm not too happy at leaving him with his daughter. He looks worse by the minute.'

'Come on, let's have a quick check and then I'll get through straight away.'

Putting his hand on her waist, Bart ushered Dempsey before him down the path and followed her through the heavy wooden door. He nodded to Vera, then bent over the big old armchair.

'Good morning, Mr Summers. I'm Dr Saville, standing in for Dr Morgan. Do you mind if I examine you a moment?' Gently, Bart took the old man's hand, then looked into his eyes. But, whereas when Dempsey had looked at Joe there had been a flicker of recognition, now the old man's eyes were unseeing, and the buzz-saw noise of his breathing seemed to echo round the tiny room, each breath a struggling effort to hold on to life.

CHAPTER FIVE

'Miss Summers —Vera—please!' Trying not to show the exasperation she was beginning to feel, Dempsey seized a pack of tissues from her bag and passed them to the weeping woman seated beside her. She glanced round the small reception area of their local hospital once more and wished for the umpteenth time that Bart would appear and bring them some news.

As soon as Bart had looked at Joe Summers, he had matters in hand, and Dempsey was surprised at the relief she had felt to have someone else take charge. It seemed only a matter of moments after Bart's arrival at the cottage that the wail of the ambulance siren warned of its approach and they were able to transfer Joe, Bart travelling with him and Dempsey driving the old man's daughter and following them to the hospital.

Though there were only two wards and a minor operating theatre, the hospital was well equipped, and always, it seemed to Dempsey, had a welcoming air, without the forbidding atmosphere that many patients felt in some bigger hospitals. As it was largely GP run, the patients usually knew the doctor looking after them and, though most of the cases were not serious, the staff at the hospital were proud of their record in dealing with some of the major problems they had faced in the past.

An occasional near-drowning when the unwary swimmer had attempted to go too far in the bay, one or two severe road crashes, sometimes an acute abdominal emergency—all had been admitted during the time that Dempsey had been the local community nurse.

She had even on one occasion seen an operation to replace part of a man's hand, torn off in a hay-baler. The tiny operating field, the delicacy of the work, culminating in a finger being used to replace his lost thumb, was as interesting as anything she'd seen in the big London hospitals during her training.

'We're very lucky to have our own local hospital.' Gently, Dempsey put her arm around Vera's shoulders. 'At least you won't have far to come, if they decide to keep your father in for a while.'

'He'll hate being in here,' Vera burbled, obviously unable to reconcile herself to the idea of anyone else coping with Joe's well-known temperament.

But before Dempsey could say any more Bart's easily recognisable figure appeared in the doorway of the medical ward, his face turned towards and his whole attention fixed on a very pretty doctor, whose long dark hair hung in a plait over her shoulder. For a moment Dempsey felt a stab of emotion, but before she could analyse what it might be Bart hurried over to them and sat down in the empty chair at Vera's side.

'Miss Summers—Vera—he's going to be all right. He's had a stroke, as you realised.' He smiled and took her hand. 'And, although it will take a little time for him to recover, it seems likely that he'll be, if not as good as new, at least able to get up and about.'

He looked over her head and smiled at Dempsey, but his eyes were troubled.

'Come on, Vera, let's go and see him, then I can drive you home.' Gently, Dempsey helped the other woman to her feet.

'I hate to ask this, Dempsey.' Bart's voice was serious, and she wheeled around, wondering what other problem could have arisen.

'What is it?' Her eyes widened as she stared at him, trying to read his expression, but she was unable to guess what he was thinking.

'Can you give me a lift back to the cottage and my car?'

'Of course; why shouldn't I. . .?' Her voice trailed away as she caught sight of the wicked glint in his eyes. Tossing her head in the air, she ushered Vera to the ward and they went inside, Vera clinging to Dempsey's arm.

Joe looked more comfortable, his green-striped pyjamas contrasting sharply with the snowy white sheets, but there was no sign of recognition as Dempsey and Vera stood at the bedside, though he opened faded blue eyes and gazed at them for a moment. His hand was still as slack as before, but when his daughter took hold Dempsey thought there was just a flicker of movement.

'Come on, Vera, we'll let him rest quietly. I'll ask the staff nurse when you can visit, and if you need a lift I'll bring you to see him.'

They checked the details of visiting hours, and

Vera took the card with the hospital telephone number, tucking it into her bag.

'Where's Dr Saville?' Both glanced around the reception area, then Dempsey caught sight of Bart, who was standing at the main entrance. Despite his resting one shoulder casually against the wooden frame of the door, and appearing completely relaxed, there was still an air of power in the lines of his body, and she paused a second, studying him and wondering what it was that made eyes gravitate in his direction. He was strikingly handsome, with his jet-black hair, strong features and dark eyes, but it was more than looks that sent a tingle through her.

'There you are.' He had heard their footsteps and swung around, then, without speaking further, they climbed into Dempsey's car, after a hasty shuffle of the papers cluttering the back seat.

The day's earlier promise of fine weather had faded, dark clouds building up to the west, and Dempsey could sense prickles of an impending storm. Though she hated to admit it, thunder made her nervous, and she drove swiftly to the Summers's cottage, ignoring the occasional murmurs of protest from Bart as she swung along the familiar narrow roads, arriving at the headland in very quick time.

'Are you sure you'll be all right?' Dempsey peered from the window of her car as Vera climbed out and stood by the gate.

'Yes, honestly, I'll ring you if I can't get to see

Dad. Thank you, both of you, for what you've done.'

'I won't say, "our pleasure",' Bart said gently, 'but I'm delighted that we were able to help. If you can't reach Sister at any time——' Dempsey blinked at the formal title, sounding strange on Bart's lips '—call me, either at the surgery or at the Fishing Smack, which is where I'm staying at present.'

'Thank you again.' Shyly Vera shook Bart's outstretched hand and hurried off, her tiny steps and wispy grey hair making her more than ever like an elderly mouse.

'Poor old thing.' Bart watched her walk away, then turned back to Dempsey, who was staring at him, bemused by the gentleness in his voice.

'What's the matter?' He raised an eyebrow at her.

'Nothing.' Hastily she cleared her throat, then went to switch on the engine. 'I shall have to miss out on our tour. . .' A sudden rumble of thunder made her wince.

'Are you all right?' he asked.

'Yes, why shouldn't I be?' Embarrassment at her weakness made her voice sharp.

'It's just that you looked pale and. . .oh, never mind.' He slid into the passenger seat and leaned forward, his folded arms resting on the dashboard. 'Are you sure you won't be able to come out to play? You know what they say—all work, etc.'

A drift of his aftershave mingled with the scents of an overgrown herb patch at the end of the

Summers's garden. Dreamily, Dempsey closed her eyes and breathed deeply. But she was startled into a heart-pounding awareness by the feel of his mouth on hers, and her eyes flicked open again. The whole of her vision was filled with him, the arch of his brows and his eyelashes, two sweeps of shadow aross his face. For just one second, her lips opened under his caress, then realisation swept through her and she pushed him away, words of protest dying in her throat as he trailed a finger over her lower lip.

'What. . .what are you dong?' She could barely get the words out, her voice harsh with surprise.

'You have a lovely mouth, Dempsey,' he whispered. 'Has no one ever told you that before?'

'No,' she said huskily, staring at him, mesmerised.

'It's full of promise, but childlike, so controlled, yet inviting.'

'I've never heard such——' she began, but she was interrupted by a roll of thunder from overhead, then a flash that lit up the heavy-bellied clouds, turning the edges to gold before they darkened once more. The crackling atmosphere of the gathering storm somehow merged with the mood inside the little car, until Dempsey felt as though every hair on her head, every nerve in her body, was at full stretch.

'I'm sorry,' she muttered nervously, 'I have to get away on my calls.'

'Yes, ma'am.' Bart sketched a salute, a smile playing about the mobile mouth, but Dempsey sensed an air of disappointment in the light-hearted words, and turned to face him.

'If I finish early,' she said shyly, 'I'll ring you at the Fishing Smack, shall I?'

'You do that. I'll get back to the surgery for now and catch up with some notes.' Without a backward glance, he climbed from her car and ran to his own, his shoulders hunched as a rattle of heavy rain began and darkened his jacket.

Not waiting to see him drive away, Dempsey set off hurriedly, her eyes peering intently through the windscreen, the wipers' monotonous beat echoing Bart's words in her mind.

'Lovely mouth, lovely mouth.' Was he attracted to her? Was he just trifling with her feelings? Was it—she tried to push the thought away, but it kept forcing itself forward—was he trying to lull her into an acceptance of the development? Of one thing she was sure; no one in the past had ever affected her so strongly.

She swerved to avoid a pool of water that had spread across the road, then straightened the car before pulling up in a street of modern bungalows, where Ben Marston lived.

Mrs Marston must have seen her arrive, for as Dempsey opened the small wooden gate, which squeaked protestingly, the front door swung back and Ben's mother ushered Dempsey into the open-plan sitting-room that stretched nearly the length of the single-storey building. It was attractively furnished, with two deep armchairs on either side of a small gas fire, a polished sideboard filling the far wall and a brightly painted yellow cupboard in one corner, where Ben crouched with a collection of cars arranged on a cardboard road plan.

'I didn't expect you to call in this weather, Sister.' The rain formed a heavy curtain down the french windows that looked out over a small garden and rolls of thunder made the radio crackle with waves of static. Mrs Marston hurried to the kitchen and spoke through the hatch as she fetched a towel and handed it to Dempsey.

'Thank you, but I'm not too wet.' Dempsey took the towel, then turned to Ben, who had watched the proceedings silently, his eyes wide.

'Now, young man——' Dempsey knelt on the floor beside him '—how about showing me some of your cars? Your collection gets bigger every time I see it.'

As she picked up some of the toys, she listened carefully while Ben described the traffic arrangement he'd made, and was relieved that there was no wheezing to be heard.

'Would you like a coffee, Sister?' Mrs Marston walked in with a tray, which she set on a low table, and Dempsey smiled gratefully at the thought. But she couldn't control a gasp as a crash of thunder was followed almost immediately by a jagged slash of lightning that lit the room.

'Goodness, what a storm!' Mrs Marston smiled as she passed mugs to Dempsey and to Ben. 'Did you see that flash?' She turned to Dempsey. 'We love the storms; there's something exciting about all that power unleashed by nature, isn't there?'

'Mm,' muttered Dempsey, her heart pounding

as the roar of the storm built to a crescendo. She couldn't believe that someone who appeared to be as nervous as Mrs Marston where her son's health was concerned could actually enjoy a storm such as the one now raging outside.

'Let's hope there aren't any fishing-boats out—that's the only worry,' Ben's mother added as she stared out of the window.

'Come on, young man.' Dempsey stood and pulled the stethoscope from her bag. 'Let's see if I can hear the air going in and out of your lungs, shall I?' Gravely Ben nodded and pulled up his T-shirt, giggling as she placed the stethoscope against his narrow ribcage.

'Well, I reckon you'll have more than enough puff to blow out your candles on your next birthday cake, don't you? Would you like to have a listen?' Without waiting for an answer, she put the ear-pieces into his ears and watched as he listened intently, his mouth open slightly, his expression absorbed.

'Now I must get on.' She drained her cup and set it on the table, packed her stethoscope away and went towards the front door.

'Are you sure you want to go out in this, Sister?' Mrs Marston stood in the hallway as Dempsey fastened the catch on her bag, ready to make a dash to her car. 'Here,' she continued, 'you must take this,' and she thrust an umbrella into Dempsey's hand.

'I have to go, more patients to see.' Dempsey decided not to say anything about the tests for the time being. Ben's mother seemed happier, and there was no need to suggest them just now.

'I wish you'd. . .' But Dempsey didn't hear the rest of the sentence. With a hurried goodbye, she ducked her head down and ran as fast as she could. Even the short sprint to the car was enough to make her feet wet, and she shivered as she started the engine and put the heater on full blast. Large puddles had settled in the roadside and the centre of the street was like a river that cascaded down towards the harbour, where the sea swirled in angry waves, white flecks of foam blown from the dark grey surface like wisps of soap, very different from the early morning sea in which she'd paddled.

I don't think there's any call that's essential at the moment. She sat lost in thought. She was going to see Philip that evening and the other two calls weren't urgent. 'Who cares about a bit of thunder? It's home to the flat and dry myself out,' she said, her voice quavering, despite her brave words.

To her relief, the engine fired first time, and she swung the car very gently, keeping it in low gear and revving the engine as she crossed the first of the large puddles spread in front of her. The rain seemed to be easing, and a watery ray of sunshine tried to force its way through the clouds. Humming to herself to keep up her spirits, Dempsey picked up speed and headed along the cliff road towards the flat. If the storm continued, much as she disliked the idea of crossing the cliff-top, she would have to go and check on her cottage and make sure that water hadn't come in through the damaged roof.

There was a splutter, and she braked hurriedly as the car suddenly swerved, taking her completely by surprise. Like a sickly bronchitic, the engine coughed, then died, and despite her efforts she was unable to coax a spark of life from it. To add to her problems, a further sweep of cloud rolled in from over the sea, and she couldn't stop herself putting her hands over her ears at the crash of thunder that followed. Hurriedly she pulled the metal slide from her hair, not to risk attracting the lightning current, then turned the key in the ignition once more.

'Come on, you. . .you. . .' Tears of frustration and panic filled her hazel eyes, her hair blew adrift, and, with a series of muttered curses, she scrambled from the car and lifted the bonnet.

Her feet were covered by freezing water and the steady downpour sent rivulets down the back of her neck, soaking her uniform dress so that it clung like a second skin. Hurriedly pulling the points free from the engine, Dempsey dried them one by one, but the engine sounded just as unhappy as she climbed back inside the car and attempted to start it.

'Where is everybody?' she moaned, peering in both directions through the cascades of water that screened the car windows. There wasn't a vehicle or person in sight; the road was deserted as far as she could see. With a muttered curse, she pulled her coat from the back seat and struggled it on over her wet dress.

Of course, my boots aren't in the car when I need them. Her thoughts tumbled in her head, matching the scrambled tendrils of her hair, which now hung around her face. Trying to get her bearings, Dempsey paused for a moment, suddenly realising how isolated some parts of the coast could be. There were no houses on this particular stretch of road, but through the swirling rain scuddies, a grey roof showed between the trees that were bending and creaking in the gusts of wind.

'The village hall.' Her words were torn away, but the sight of a solid building pushed aside her fear for the moment, and she seized her bag and struggled along the shingle path, through a narrow wooden gate and hurried thankfully into the doorway of the granite hut at the top of the hill. It was deserted, but the sound of the rain drumming on a solid roof was music to her ears. Going to a large cupboard in the corner of the porch, she found a one-bar electric fire and pulled it gratefully from among the clutter.

Everything smelt damp, but Dempsey hardly noticed. Plugging in the fire in the small kitchen, she took off her dress, hung it over a chair, slipped off her shoes and then went to the sink and filled the electric kettle. It seemed an age before the water boiled, and she was shivering, in spite of the comparative warmth of her uniform coat. With a feeling of relief, she made herself coffee and warmed her hands on the mug as she crouched in front of the single glowing bar of the fire.

'What a climate!' She gazed at the narrow window in disgust. The thunder had eased, with just a few rumbles in the distance now, but the rain was as heavy as ever, and she settled herself for a long wait. She knew only the basics about car engines, and would have to rely on help from the local garage, if and when she could get to a telephone. Her chill gradually eased and, taking the coffee-cup in her hand, she wandered into the main body of the hall, her attention drawn to the model layout of the proposed development.

The shape of the bay was immediately recognisable, and Dempsey studied it with interest. As a matter of principle, she had refused to look at it before, but in her present solitary state it seemed an ideal opportunity to judge what the opposition had to offer.

She had to admit that it was a very attractive model. A row of houses crept along one edge, all of them coloured as though trimmed with local stone. There was no evidence of amusement arcades or funfairs, such as she had pictured. Merely a hotel complex, which complemented the layout of houses, with a leisure park that led down to a boating marina and small pier, taking in the area that was now used by the few fishing-boats left in Penmawtha.

'I must say,' she whispered to herself, 'it could be a lot worse.' She swallowed the last of her coffee and went towards the kitchen, encouraged by a break in the clouds, but her footsteps were halted as the main door was flung back.

'Are you all right?' Without waiting for an

answer, Bart hurried towards her and seized her in a hug so fierce that Dempsey was forced to protest.

'I saw your car, empty by the roadside, and I couldn't think what had happened.' As he murmured the words, he smoothed her damp hair and patted her back, finally pushing her away at arm's length to look into her face.

'Of course I'm all right. My car was stuck in the rain and I came here for shelter.' Embarrassed at the intensity of his stare, and remembering her state of undress, Dempsey edged towards the kitchen. 'This isn't New York or London, you know. The fact that my car wouldn't go is probably the worst thing that's likely to happen to me. It's usually very reliable, but the wet proved too much for it. As I was soaked and this was nearest shelter, I came here to dry off.' She turned in the kitchen doorway and flashed a brilliant smile in his direction, determined not to show how touched she was by his concern. 'So there was no need for you to worry.'

He didn't answer, but paused, tension reaching out from every pore. His hair was seal-dark, smooth against the well-shaped head, his eyes half closed. The beautiful suede jacket was darkened by the rain, but he looked unaware of anything except herself. With two swift strides, he reached her side.

'You are the most aggravating. . .' His voice trailed away as he seized her shoulders and pulled her close, his mouth descending on hers. There was no gentleness in his kiss. It was a fierce, demanding pressure that seemed to tear Dempsey's heart from her. She froze, stunned into immobility, then the texture of his mouth changed, softening, moving over her lips so that despite herself she responded, her arms reaching behind his head, her hands entwining in the thick, springy hair which clung to the nape of his neck, still damp from the storm. The thrumming of the rain had started again on the roof, echoing the beat of Dempsey's heart, but then a sudden crack of thunder made her start and she pulled away from Bart's enfolding arms, her eyes wide, her mouth bruised but pulsing with the intensity of their kiss.

With an impatient shrug, Bart ran his hand through his hair and turned away from her.

'For God's sake go and put some proper clothes on,' he muttered huskily, 'or I might forget that you're a professional colleague and do something we both regret.'

Dempsey gasped as she looked down, for her coat had fallen open and the tiny bra and panties were more revealing than any bikini. Not speaking, she whirled into the kitchen and pushed the door shut behind her. Her hands were shaking as she quickly struggled into the still damp uniform dress and pulled on her shoes. Whatever was she thinking of? Even though Bart had instigated the kiss, her response had taken her completely by surprise, and she trembled at the thought of facing him again.

Raking her finges through the tangle of her hair, she switched off the fire, checked around the kitchen, took a deep breath and walked out into the main body of the hall, her head held high, her heart racing as she went to meet Bart's enigmatic gaze.

CHAPTER SIX

DEMPSEY sighed with pleasure and leaned back against the soft leather upholstery. The sensation of luxury in the large, comfortable Mercedes helped to soothe her jangled nerves as she tried to forget the tensions of the previous hour. For the first part of the journey, she stared out through the windscreen, not wanting to face Bart after their kiss, but now that they had been driving for several minutes she had relaxed enough to risk a glance from the corner of her eye at his stern expression.

They were both silent, lost in their own thoughts. Several times, Dempsey tried to say something, but each time she went to speak the memory of how she had returned Bart's kiss, and her body's instant reaction, brought a flush to her face, and eventually she pretended to doze, only sitting upright as the car glided to a halt.

'Would you like a cup of coffee?' Nervously, Dempsey bit her lip and turned towards the driving seat.

'You get yourself dry. I'll see to your car and telephone you later.' Bart's voice was cool as he stretched across her lap and flung open the passenger door.

'You don't have to bother; I can call the garage. . .' Dempsey began.

'Run along; I'll see to it.' Leaning forward, Bart gently flicked the end of her nose with his finger, a half-smile creasing his face as he waited for her to leave.

Not sure if she felt relief or disappointment that he wasn't stopping, Dempsey ran along the path to her flat, not bothering to avoid the puddles that were full of fallen rainbows in the light from a brilliant blue sky, where the clouds were now being chased away by a strong breeze.

She sniffed in appreciation of the newly washed smell of the earth, and hurried inside, taking off her coat and dress and kicking aside her shoes.

Reaching into the refrigerator on the way past, she poured herself a glass of wine. Her reflection drew a grimace of horror as she went into the bathroom, her hair a tangled mass, cheeks shining, the freckles that she hated so much standing out against her skin. She turned on the taps, then poured in an extravagant amount of scented bath oil, before going into the sitting-room and switching on the answering machine.

'Hi, Dempsey, it's Philip. If you're out this way, call in for a coffee. No rush—Mum's seen to all the necessary bits and pieces for today.' The machine beeped, then started again.

'Hello, Dempsey, I thought you might like to know, things look more hopeful with regard to Jenny. Oh. . .' there was a pause '. . .Blast, I forgot to say it's David Morgan. I'll ring again later.'

'Hi, Miss Dempsey, if I don't see you before, how about a drink this evening? We can combine business with pleasure.' The sound of Bart's voice sent shivers down Dempsey's spine.

I wonder when he put that message on tape, she thought, running into the bathroom as the bath threatened to overflow. She stripped off her underwear and sank into the bubbles, resting back with a sigh of contentment.

Picking up her glass from the bathroom stool, she raised it in a silent toast, then took a large swallow.

'I'd like to hide here all day,' she sighed at the clouds of steam drifting towards the ceiling.

The sound of the front doorbell woke her, and she struggled up from the cooling water, unable to remember for a moment where she was or what was happening. As she reached across to the stool, her watch showed her she had been in the water for nearly an hour and, with a shiver, she seized a large bath-towel and wrapped it around herself, tucking the ends in securely above her breasts.

'Yes, who is it?' She stood impatiently inside the door as there was no reply, then carefully slipped the latch and peered round the opening.

'Oh, no,' she sighed. 'What are you doing here?' Her hair, which she had clipped up at the back, hung in damp tendrils around her face, and she flushed with embarrassment as she recognised her visitor.

'Well, there's a nice welcome, I must say.' Bart raised his eyebrows and whistled softly, looking at the towel. 'I merely called round to bring you the keys and to tell you that your car is fixed. But I can take a hint—I'll be on my way.'

'Oh, just a minute.' Hastily Dempsey swung the door wide. 'I'm sorry; I didn't mean to sound so offhand. I—er—I fell asleep in the bath.'

'I've left my car by the village hall, and I was hoping you could take me back there to pick it up. But it's obviously a bad time. I'll find my own way.'

'Don't be silly. It's the least I can do to take you, after you've gone to all that trouble. Sit there and I'll slip into something more comfortable.' Dempsey giggled at the cliché, holding firmly to the edges of the towel.

'Please do, I can't wait here with a quiet mind with you looking like that.'

Her face coloured more deeply at the implication in Bart's words as she hurried into the bedroom and shut the door. It took her only moments to pull on jeans and a striped T-shirt, brush her hair and smooth on a trace of lipstick. Picking up her shoulder-bag, she went back into the sitting-room.

'That was quick,' Bart smiled approvingly. His expression was friendly but no more, giving no hint of what had taken place earlier. Quickly he stood and opened the door and walked out behind her. Again he said little as Dempsey drove them back to the village hall to collect his car.

He seemed lost in thought, sometimes clearing his throat as though to speak, then giving a barely perceptible shrug of his shoulders. He had taken off his jacket and was now dressed in just the

plain cream shirt, striped tie and casual trousers.
The breadth of his shoulders was emphasised by
the material which clung across his back and
tapered to his slim waist; Dempsey had to concentrate hard on her driving to control the desire she
felt to reach out and touch him.

'What are you doing for the rest of the day?'
Unable to bear the silence any longer, and worried
that Bart might be aware of her covert glances, she
spoke in a voice that sounded brittle and artificial
to her ears.

'Well, my plans for the day have been knocked
sideways. First of all, I see you dancing about like
a nymph at the water's edge, then we have to
rush Joe Summers into hospital, then there was
the problem with your car. I'm beginning to
wonder if I can stand the pace in this sleepy
Cornish village.'

'You don't have to make fun.' Huffily, Dempsey
pulled up beside Bart's car and turned to face him,
her colour heightened with annoyance.

'I'm not making fun,' Bart said softly. 'I would
never make fun of anything dear to you. But you
have to admit——' he laughed suddenly, a joyous
sound that filled the car '—it has been a hectic
morning in all sorts of ways.'

'I suppose you're right,' she agreed.

'Anyway, it's lunchtime. Where can we get
ourselves something to eat?'

'Haven't you anything else you'd rather do?'
Much as she longed to be with him, Dempsey was
doubtful of the wisdom of spending so much time
in Bart's company. The morning had shown her

only too well how attractive she found him, and it
was short-sighted to try to ignore the strength of
her feelings.

'Now, I know there are no more calls—I
checked at the surgery. You promised to show me
around, and I'm starving after all the activity of
the morning. And. . .' he paused, a wicked glint
in his eyes '. . .I promise not to lay a finger on
you.'

It's your lips I'm worried about, thought
Dempsey, surprising herself. 'Right, we'll go
along the coast a little way, have a real pasty and
cider lunch, then I'll start my guided tour.' She
looked at him. 'If that's all right with you?' she
finished uncertainly.

'Around here you're the boss. Lead on! One
stipulation—my car.' Not stopping to see her
reaction, Bart climbed from her vehicle, walked
across to the Mercedes and held the passenger
door open. The sun had completely dried the
clouds of the morning and was shimmering in the
few pools of water still lying in the road. The sea
had turned to green, blue and turquoise. Though,
further out at the edge of the bay, the white tops
on the waves betrayed the remnants of the storm
that had otherwise disappeared.

'A country road, a pretty girl, a comfortable car,
a pretty girl, a sunny day, a pretty girl, what more
could anyone ask?' Bart sang out as they drove
swiftly along the coast road, seeing very little
other traffic, which Dempsey thought was just as
well, as the car seemed to fill the width of some of
the lanes they went through.

The hedgerows were dotted with splashes of colour, the yellow of the wild snapdragon mixed with pink campion and the tiny blue eyes of the speedwell flower.

They soon arrived at the public house that Dempsey had in mind—a low-slung building, scarcely visible from the roadside, its granite slabs merging into the background. As they sat outside, eating a simple lunch of the promised pasties and cider brewed on the premises, Dempsey thought that the orchard at the rear of the garden looked too overgrown to produce enough apples worthy of the name to make the deceptively strong drink.

'I think one pint is more than enough for me,' declared Bart, and he and Dempsey sat in companionable silence, both enjoying the warmth of the sun on their upturned faces. The only sound in the still air came from a courageous blackbird which hovered around them as Dempsey threw the remaining crumbs of pastry on the ground. She watched it through half-closed eyes, noticing how the blue-black of its wings matched the glint of Bart's hair in the sunlight.

'What are you going to do when your research is finished?' Straightening in her chair, Dempsey took a sip from her glass.

'What I'd really like. . .' Bart paused and stared at her. 'It sounds a bit far-fetched.'

'Go on,' she invited.

'I'd like to do more research, but in the field of neurology. Look into the possibility of transplants for nervous diseases.'

'Well, nerves can be grafted in some cases now, can't they?'

'Yes, but I was thinking of the larger nerve disorders.' He sat forward, his expression intense. 'Just think if the time should come when someone like Philip, for example, could have a transplant, graft—call it what you will—and be able to walk again. Or, after a stroke, if the damaged pathways from the brain could be replaced.'

Dempsey shivered. 'It makes a good theory, but it sounds—I don't know. . .'

'I suppose there could be lots of problems, but no more than any other form of grafting. Regeneration of nerves would be the ideal, of course. But I think that's all far in the future, unfortunately.' Bart sat in silence for a moment. 'Anyway, come along; we can't sit here all day.'

Standing in front of her chair, he seized her hands and pulled her to her feet. They stood face to face, barely inches apart, but Dempsey was unable to read Bart's expression behind his dark glasses. She was aware of the noise of her breathing, her hands shaking slightly as she freed them hurriedly from his clasp.

'What's next on the agenda?' Turning away, she straightened the two wrought-iron chairs and placed the plates and glasses tidily together.

'I'm in your hands. Are we going to have a look around the local beauty spots, spend an afternoon on the beach? What would you like to do?'

Dempsey thought for a moment. It was a novel experience for her to try to see her home with a tourist's eyes. The thought crossed her mind that, if she made it too attractive, Bart and his father would be more inclined than ever to want to build the leisure park there. But, on the other hand, her deep pride and feeling for her birthplace and the home of her family for many generations wouldn't let her be less than honest.

'Penny for 'em?' Bart took her arm and swung her to face him once more.

'Trying to decide where to go first. Are you interested in—er—say, Cornish tin mining?'

'I'm not going underground.' Emphatically, Bart shook his head. 'And certainly not on such a lovely afternoon.'

'I didn't mean that, silly.' Amused by Bart's expression, Dempsey rested her hand on his arm. But she pulled away sharply at the shock that went through her as she touched him.

'Come on; if you can't decide, I must,' he said. 'Let's go to the beach you were on this morning. Have you got a swimsuit with you?'

'The water will be freezing,' she warned.

'I'm game if you are.'

'Right. It's very near my flat; I can call in and collect everything I need.'

With a face full of mischief, Bart took her hand and ran towards the Mercedes. They drove to the flat, where Dempsey changed into a plain black swimsuit and yellow towelling dress, and then down to the cove so quickly that she barely had time to catch her breath.

The beach was nearly deserted, the only other occupants a family of four, the two children busily patting piles of sand into shape, and a group of teenagers playing a noisy game of ball at the far end.

'Last one in's a chicken!' Suddenly shy, Dempsey pulled off her wrap and raced down towards the waves, but she was easily overtaken by Bart's tanned, athletic figure in a pair of snug pale blue shorts as he dived cleanly in at the water's edge. Gasping with shock at the cold as she followed suit, Dempsey struck out in an overarm crawl, ducking her head under the incoming waves, but, strong swimmer that she was, she was unable to keep up with Bart's powerful strokes, and soon his dark head surfaced in front of her.

'I told you it would be freezing,' she laughed as Bart pretended to shiver, rubbing his hands on his arms, before rolling over and disappearing under the water in a backward dive.

'I'd call this healthy.' He reappeared in front of her, grinning like a small boy, his eyelashes fringed with drops from the sea.

Treading water, she paddled alongside. 'Where did you learn to swim?' she asked.

'Believe it or not, I first learnt when I was a kid in Yorkshire. If you think this water's cold, you ought to try plunging into the North Sea some time.'

'This is cold enough for me. Come on—race you.' Feeling more carefree than she had for many months, Dempsey set off towards the beach, her head turning to the side with each stroke, her legs kicking out strongly behind her. She strode out through the small waves at the edge of the sand

and hurried to the gaily coloured towels, turning to face the water as she flopped down.

But she sat up again sharply when she realised there was no sign of Bart. Looking up and down the beach, jumping to her feet and peering towards the bay, she felt her heart begin to pound with dread. Where was he? He was a much stronger swimmer than she was; he should have arrived back before her. But he was nowhere in sight. Some currents could be tricky, but there wasn't usually anything to worry about on this bit of coast. Slinging her towel round her shoulders, Dempsey set off at an awkward run towards the family she'd seen earlier.

'Have you seen my friend—the one who was swimming with me?' Her breath rasped in her throat so that she could barely say the words.

'We saw you out in the water together just now.' Sensing her anxiety, the man jumped to his feet and stood beside her. 'In fact, I remarked to my wife what a pair of strong swimmers you were, didn't I, love? I said you must know these waters well. But we haven't seen. . .'

But Dempsey didn't wait to hear any more. With a muttered word of thanks, she ran down to the water's edge and started to walk into the waves. Her heart was beating so fast, she felt sick. Bart could have had cramp, perhaps they'd swum too soon after their meal, or he'd been caught by seaweed, he could have. . . She thrust the thought away.

'Hey, where are you going?' A strong grip

seized her elbow and she whirled around, her feet
floundering in the surf at the edge of the beach.

'Where are you going?' Bart repeated the
question.

'Where have you been?' Demspey's voice was
shrill.

'I've been swimming back to the beach, what do
you think I've been doing?'

'You stupid——' Almost in tears, she hurried
away and sat down on the sand.

'Dempsey, Miss Dempsey, what is it?' Gently
Bart put a finger under her chin and raised her
face towards him. 'Why are you so upset?'

Swallowing hard, Dempsey pulled her face
away. If she told Bart how terrified she'd been
when she thought him missing, he might guess at
the strength of her rapidly growing feelings. And
that was something she didn't dare reveal to
herself, let alone to him.

'I thought for a minute you'd done something
stupid, such as got cramp. I was worried that we
might have to send out a search party, that's all.'
Tossing her head, she seized her towel and began
rubbing briskly at her hair. Not for anything could
she betray how she felt. She managed a shaky
laugh. 'I should have guessed that Bart Saville
wouldn't allow himself to get into difficulties!'

'I swam part of the way under water and came
up near those rocks.' Quickly Bart sat down beside
her. 'I had no idea it would worry you so much,
and I'm sorry.'

'It wasn't that I was particularly upset, it's just

that I do feel a certain amount of responsibility, in the same way that I would for any visitor.'

'Ouch!' winced Bart, but he didn't say any more, just lay back on his towel and closed his eyes. The trickles of moisture that ran down his chest drew Dempsey's gaze despite herself, fixing her attention on the strong, supple body so near hers—broad shoulders, neat waist and flat stomach and long, powerful legs, all coloured a rich, even tan. Sitting forward, she hugged her knees, and stared determinedly out to sea. It wouldn't do for Bart to catch her looking at him in the way that she was.

But, though her eyes were fixed on the horizon, her thoughts kept mulling over the last few days. It was difficult to believe that she had known Bart for little more than a week. The impact he had made in that time was greater than she could ever have suspected when she'd first seen him.

She had never been one to analyse her emotions in the past, usually content to accept things as they happened. But her thoughts and feelings had suffered such turmoil since Bart's entry into her life that they frightened her. She glanced at him once more, then looked away again. What is it the poets say? she thought. That the eyes are the windows of the soul? Not for anything did she want her eyes to betray to Bart how she felt.

A sudden chill breeze lifted the hair at the nape of her neck, making her shiver. They'd not spoken, and for some little while Dempsey thought that Bart was asleep. But then she had felt his eyes upon her, and determined to remain silent. However, the cool breeze forced her to pick up her belongings and suggest they make a move.

'I'm ready.' With his usual masculine grace, Bart stood up and held out a hand to help her to her feet. But she ignored it, afraid she would betray how she felt, though she suffered misgivings at the sight of the frown that caused Bart to turn away.

'I'll take you to your car, then I must dash. I have to sort out several matters for my father and it will probably take most of the evening.' His tone was cool and crisp.

'That's fine,' Dempsey shrugged. 'I didn't expect to monopolise all your time.'

They collected their towels and clothes, Dempsey carefully folding hers and shaking the sand from her sandals. It was a five-minute drive, and Bart waved a brief goodbye, hardly pausing long enough to let her get out of the car.

'See you in surgery on Monday,' called Dempsey, but he merely waved and drove off with a spin of his wheels, leaving her to stand forlornly by her car.

CHAPTER SEVEN

'I WOULDN'T want another week like that.' Dempsey took a mug of coffee from Rita's outstretched hand and sank thankfully into the chair that her friend pushed towards her. 'I was really shocked about Joe Summers, weren't you?'

Rita nodded, shuffling through the papers on her desk, muttering with exasperation when she couldn't find the form she was looking for.

'I thought I had the post-mortem result somewhere, but I can't see it at the moment.'

'I'm not sure why they wanted one. Did Bart say?' asked Dempsey.

'He thought it would be better as he wasn't actually Joe's GP, and hadn't been treating him for long. From what I remember, the cause of death was another stroke.'

'I know it sounds a bit hard-hearted,' Dempsey said quietly, 'but in the circumstances it was probably for the best. He would have hated being completely helpless, and Vera couldn't have looked after someone in that state. Though what she'll do with herself, now that her father's gone, I can't imagine.'

'I didn't realise Joe was quite that old.' Rita drained her mug and put it on the desk. 'I know we've got all his details in his notes, but I've never really taken much notice.'

'I guessed he must have been getting on a bit, because of course he was a friend of my grandfather. It will certainly be funny not to have his crabby old face around the village, that's for sure.' Dempsey stretched her arms above her head and sighed. 'Changing the subject, has Philip been in touch again? I'm very worried about his emotional state. He was so depressed the last time I saw him.'

'Well, it's understandable, isn't it?' said Rita.

'Oh, yes, of course it is. But it's only recently that he's seemed so low in spirits. After all, the accident happened quite some time ago. I don't really know what anyone can do. He absolutely refuses to go away for any sort of rehabilitation and, let's face it, his previous interests were rather limited. All he ever wanted to do was carry on with the farm.' Dempsey swallowed. 'And I've heard that his cousin has come to help out with the heavy work, which won't have made Philip feel any better. Do you know——' her voice rose in a squeak of protest '—he even told me not to keep calling round? That hurt me. We've always been such good friends as well as patient and nurse.'

'Dempsey, you are an old innocent sometimes, aren't you?' Rita smiled.

'Eh? What do you mean?' Dempsey took off her hat and threw it on the desk. 'Phew, it's hotter than ever this morning.'

'Philip has always been—well, you know. . .' Rita paused.

'If you're suggesting what I think you're

suggesting,' Dempsey said vehemently, 'it's a load of rubbish.'

'Oh, yeah? Well, I think it could have a lot to do with his problem.'

'Rita, that's awful.' Dempsey sat back on the seat, her face pale. 'How can I look after him properly if he won't see me because of some silly fancy?'

But, before Rita could answer, the main door swung back and both women straightened as Bart appeared.

Allowing for the heat of the morning, he was dressed in a snowy white short-sleeved shirt and lightweight pale grey trousers. He looked so cool and fresh and completely at ease that Dempsey's heart turned over with longing at the sight of him.

'Good morning, ladies, any of that coffee left?' During the previous couple of weeks, his behaviour towards Dempsey had been that of professional colleague and friend. He was pleasant and charming, eager to ask Dempsey's opinion on all subjects connected with the practice, and happy to go out for a drink or coffee when they'd finished work. But the increasing intimacy that had so frightened yet thrilled her had gone, and, although she knew she was being unreasonable in her disappointment, she couldn't help feeling let down.

Rita poured coffee and stirred in two spoonfuls of sugar.

'Just as I like it. Rita, you're a genius, the way you remember everything.' Rita blushed, then turned her head away, picking up a file and shuffling through the pages.

'If it's not being too nosy, what was all the intense discussion when I came in just now?' queried Bart.

'I was remarking to Rita that I wouldn't want to go through the past week again.' Dempsey took her cup and refilled it, then picked up her hat, preparatory to going to her office.

'There were some aspects in which I wouldn't mind a replay,' Bart said softly, leaning against the edge of the desk and staring at her over the rim of his coffee-mug. 'Are you about to take me sightseeing again this weekend?'

'If you like.' Dempsey couldn't have sounded more offhand, but her heart began its rapid tattoo at the thought of spending time with Bart. Then she paused. 'Oh, I can't. Rita and I are getting the Morgan house clean and tidy, ready for when Dr Morgan gets back.'

'I'd forgotten he was coming home today. It's good news about his daughter, isn't it?'

'Yes, wonderful.'

'What's happened?' Rita poked her head up from her notebook. She tutted. 'I should be a doctor—my writing gets worse every time I look at it!'

'Dr Morgan's daughter has a contusion and swelling of the spinal cord. Very nasty, of course, but she should make a good recovery,' Dempsey told her, eyes shining.

'Didn't you know about it?' Bart said curiously.

'No, not till now. Well, at least there's been one piece of good news this week.'

But Dempsey wasn't listening, for an unwelcome thought had crossed her mind. She turned to face Bart. 'Does that mean you'll be leaving, if David is coming back to take over the practice again?' She didn't realise how horrified she sounded until Rita looked at her, surprise all over her round, pleasant face.

Bart took Dempsey's hand. 'Don't say you'll miss me,' he teased.

'I—it's not that,' she stammered. 'It's just. . .' Her voice trailed away and she moved back from the desk.

But Bart was still holding her hand, and without making an issue of it Dempsey couldn't think of a way to break free. Especially as Rita was watching them closely.

'Are you leaving Penmawtha?' she repeated.

'Not yet. I expect Dr Morgan will be glad of a back-up in the practice, and I still have a lot to arrange with regard to the leisure park.'

'The plans haven't been passed, have they?' Dempsey squealed.

'No, not finally, but it does look as though there won't be any problems in getting planning permission. After all,' Bart added, smiling at her gently, 'that is the real reason for my stay.'

'You'll get them passed over my dead body!' Snatching up her hat and medical bag, Dempsey marched through to her office and slammed the door behind her.

How dared he? How *dared* he? Behaving

towards her like a friend, pretending a general
interest in the village, asking her to show him
around, and all the time with his mind still fixed
on the development. How could she have been so
naïve as not to realise? And to think that she was
on the verge of falling in love with him! She
paused, aghast. She wasn't, was she? Of course
not. It was just. . .just. . .physical attraction.

She threw her files on the desk, not bothering
to retrieve the ones that slithered to the floor, and
picked up the telephone with a shaking hand. But
she replaced the receiver after a moment, not sure
who she should ring or even what she should do.

They had seemed to think as one in so many
ways. During a visit to the local museum, a
museum started by Dempsey's great-grandfather
and full of references to her family, Bart had
remarked how secure she must feel in having so
much of her family history all around her. He had
been impressed by it, she was sure. The photographs of the old mine workings, the various
descriptions of the machinery, small working
models, tin-smelting marks, all of them associated
with her in some way.

One day they visited a small boatyard and saw
a boat named *Dempsey* after one of her relatives.
Though she had to admit to herself, if not to him,
that the yard was a sorry picture now compared
with how busy it had been in the past. And,
throughout it all, Bart had given her the
impression that he understood how much it meant
to her, that things should stay as they were. What
a hope!

Even more worrying was the effect he had had on her senses, the tumult inside every time she saw him, the delight she had felt when he sought her company. She sank back in her chair, tears of rage and frustration quivering on the edge of her lashes, and switched on the intercom.

'Rita, I'm going out to do some calls. I know they're not really booked for this morning, but I want to catch up with a few I missed earlier in the week.'

'Are you all right?' Rita's concern was apparent, even through the machine's tinny echo.

'Yes, I'm fine. Has Bart gone?' Dempsey lowered her voice.

'He's in his office.'

Packing the few dressings and extra notes she needed, Dempsey hurried from her office and crept past the reception area, warning Rita to silence by putting her finger to her lips. But just as she opened the main door, a familiar voice called out from behind her.

'Dempsey! Sister! Could you come here for a moment?'

Swearing under her breath, Dempsey spun on her heel, tilted her hat forward at a more defiant angle and strode into Bart's office.

'Sit down, please, Dempsey.'

'I don't think——'

'Please—sit down.'

With poor grace, Dempsey perched on the edge of the chair and hugged her bag to her chest.

Bart looked up. His expression was difficult to read, for he sat with his back to the window, where the sunlight streamed in, showing up the dust motes dancing in the air and making a patchwork of light and dark on the shabby brown carpet. Garden scents drifted in through the open window as the sun rapidly dried the remaining dew on the plants.

'Right.' He pushed some papers into a tidy heap and leaned forward, his arms resting on the desk. 'What's upset you?'

'I don't know what you're talking about,' Dempsey muttered resentfully.

'Come along, don't insult me by being less than honest. You're upset, and I want to know why.'

'I don't think you've been very honest in your dealings with me,' she retorted.

'Oh, in what way?'

Dempsey remained silent.

'If you remember, Dempsey, a couple of weeks ago we agreed that we would try to show each other our differing points of view. You would take me round the village, saying why it's important to you that the development doesn't take place.'

'Yes, but——'

'Let me finish.' He picked up a pencil and turned it over and over in his fingers. 'I've always tried to be fair. You've known all along my reason for being here, and I don't feel I've misled you at any time.' He smiled, showing a flash of white teeth.

'If anyone should be confused, it should be me. I thought you liked my company, were happy to spend time with me, even—dare I say it?—— ' his voice dropped a tone '—even enjoyed my kisses, few though they've been. I promise you, Dempsey, if there's definite news of the development, I'll tell you straight away. I haven't any reason to keep it quiet.' He stood up and walked around the desk. 'But you must have guessed this anyway. What really made you so upset just now?'

'I thought you were going behind my back.' Dempsey gazed out through the window, not really seeing the antics of the sparrows who were quarrelling in the tree outside. All she could think was that she mustn't betray to Bart how she felt.

He obviously thought of her as a pleasant companion and colleague, despite the occasional kiss. She felt—what did she feel? Did she love him? Was she merely attracted by his sheer masculinity? Whatever it was, it was making her very vulnerable, and she mustn't be other than strong.

'Anyway, that's enough of that for the moment. I want to be very boring and talk about work. Have you seen Mrs Bagstock this week?'

Dempsey sat up. This was safer ground.

'Yes, I saw her on Tuesday. Her leg doesn't seem to be much better.'

'I suppose it's understandable.' Bart strolled towards the window and paused, tapping his teeth with his pencil. 'She's nearly eighty and obviously hasn't the reserves of a younger person.'

'The dressings don't seem to have helped at all.'

'I don't think her ulcer is suitable for grafting; all her skin is so fragile.' Bart looked thoughtful. 'There is a new treatment, based on growth hormone. Have you come across it?'

'No.' Dempsey shook her head.

'It's still rather experimental and is also very expensive, but I think it might be worth a try. Leave it with me and I'll look into it.'

'Shall I carry on with the vaseline gauze as before?' Dempsey pulled her work-list from her bag and scribbled busily.

'Yes, that's probably best. The other patient I'm concerned about is Philip. His emotional state is worrying.' Bart sat astride an upright chair and rested his arm along the back.

'I was going to speak to you about him. I've a horrible suspicion he's given up.'

'Well, we can't let that happen. I hope you think this is a good idea.' Bart walked to the cupboard in the corner of the room and took out a long leather case. Unzipping it along its length, he pulled out a piece of curved polished wood with a leather band around the centre.

'What is it?' Puzzled, Dempsey leaned forward.

'It's the bow from an archery set. I thought Philip might like to try it. I'm no expert, but I was assured when I bought it that it's suitable for a paraplegic to use.' Bart looked almost shy as he waited for her comments.

'Oh, Bart, what a lovely idea. If Philip doesn't like it, he wants shaking.' Carefully, Dempsey ran her hand along the length of polished wood, savouring its clean, linseed smell.

'If I suggest it as a form of treatment, he might try it. Doctor's orders and all that,' Bart laughed.

'You're very nice sometimes, aren't you?' Dempsey looked at him shyly.

'Only sometimes? And that's not what you were saying a few moments ago. I felt I was next door to being the devil incarnate.' Bart pulled a face. 'Anyway, off you go. I want to get all the prescriptions and forms up to date before David Morgan comes back, and you're distracting me.' His voice still held a laugh, but Dempsey could have sworn that there was an edge of seriousness in his tone.

She walked towards the door. 'I must get on. I want to persuade Philip to go for a drive this afternoon—somewhere like Penhelly sands.' She paused, fingering the door handle nervously. 'Bart, I'm sorry about this morning—I don't know why I got so upset.'

'No problem.' Bart waved without looking up, but Dempsey felt more reassured as she hurried from the surgery and went outside to her car.

'I think we've done a good job here, even if I do say so myself.' Rita wrung out the dishcloth before hanging it over the edge of the sink, and wiped her hand across her forehead. 'I tell you what, it's much easier doing my filing and notes than sorting out David Morgan's place.' She frowned sympathetically. 'You could tell he and Mary left in a hurry.'

Dempsey and Rita had been busy for nearly two hours cleaning and tidying the converted farmhouse where the Morgans lived. With its four bedrooms, large sitting-room, study and old-fashioned kitchen, they had had to work hard, and now they sank back on the chairs in the kitchen and looked around with very nearly matching expressions of smug satisfaction.

Everything gleamed. There were fresh flowers and pot-pourri in all the rooms, the perfume blending with the smell of lavender polish; plates of cold meat and salad sat ready in the fridge, and Rita had laid a tray of cups and saucers ready for tea or coffee when Dr Morgan and his wife returned.

'I wouldn't want to do it too often—certainly not in this temperature, anyway,' Dempsey sighed, fanning her face with a folded newspaper. 'How about helping ourselves to a cold drink and then making a move?'

'Good idea, but don't mess up my nice tidy kitchen.' Rita laughed at Dempsey's expression of disgust as she filled two glasses with lemon squash and passed one across the table. 'I love this old house, don't you?' Rita drank thirstily. 'You can just imagine bringing up a family here.'

'I wonder why David and Mary had only the one?' mused Dempsey.

'Don't know.' Rita stretched wearily. 'Come on, let's get away so they find the place as a surprise. I hope they appreciate it.'

'Of course they will. Mary is one of the nicest people. Oh,' Dempsey said fiercely, 'let's pray that Jenny makes a good recovery. I think it would nearly kill the Morgans if she doesn't.'

'Come on, on your feet, and don't be so morbid.' Rita seized Dempsey by the arm and pulled her from the chair. 'What are you doing for the rest of the day?'

'Going to see Philip,' Dempsey said quickly.

'Do you think it's wise?' Rita rinsed out the two glasses and polished them briskly before hanging the tea-towel on a rail by the big red Aga.

'Yes, I've thought about it very carefully, and there's no way that I can avoid seeing him. Who will take care of all the personal details if I don't? So. . .' Dempsey rubbed at an imaginary smear on the table with the edge of the towel, then walked towards the door. '. . .So I'm going there as though he hasn't acted in any way different from usual.'

'It might work. Are you coming over for lunch tomorrow?'

'Yes, please. You know I can't resist your home-cooking.' Rita laughed and quickly the two friends ran down the shallow steps from the front door, pulling it shut behind them.

'I'll take the key and leave it at the surgery as it's on my way, shall I, Dempsey?'

'If you don't mind. I want to go home and change from this elegant outfit——' Dempsey gestured at her patched T-shirt and cut-off jeans '—and I shall insist on taking Philip for a drive somewhere this afternoon.'

Not only was she anxious to see Philip before their relationship became strained, but she was also eager to see his reaction to the present from Bart. Perhaps it would be enough to stimulate Philip's interest and help to lift some of his depression. Though it seemed a lot to ask of a sport. Instinctively she realised that Bart would not want his gift made public knowledge—at least for the time being.

At the flat, she made herself a sandwich, had a quick shower and changed into a pretty sundress in her favourite apple-green, afterwards driving swiftly to Philip's home. Patchy cloud was shielding the sun by the time she arrived, making the day much cooler and more pleasant.

'What are you doing here?' Philip's manner at first was abrupt, but Dempsey bustled round the little bungalow, ignoring his sullen expression. Pity stirred her heart at the shadows under his eyes and the waxiness of his skin.

'I'm at a loose end this afternoon, and thought you might fancy a drive and, at the same time, keep me company,' she told him.

'Could do, I suppose.'

'Great.' Pretending an enthusiasm she didn't really feel, Dempsey pushed Philip out to her car and placed the plank across to the passenger seat. Swiftly Philip wriggled along it, then tucked his hands under his knees and lifted his legs inside as Dempsey folded the wheelchair and packed it in the open hatchback area.

'Have you any preferences, Phil, or shall we make it a mystery tour?'

'Whatever you like.' He pushed himself back more comfortably, and, though Dempsey's fingers itched to help him, she stopped herself in time, looking straight ahead as she switched on the ignition and started the engine.

'Right, mystery tour it is.' What he needs is not only a change of scene, but to see some different faces, she thought, as she drove carefully down the winding road from the farm, reaching the cove soon after.

At first Philip was silent, staring out at the passing scenery, his expression rigid. But as the car ate up the miles he gradually became more animated and was soon remarking on the ripeness of the wheatfields, noticing plants in the hedge-row, and didn't seem upset at the sight of a large tractor that they followed for several minutes before Dempsey was able to overtake it.

'That's the same sort as the one which caused your accident, isn't it?' She held her breath as she asked the question, but Philip nodded matter-of-factly, and Dempsey sighed with relief.

'Here we are—civilisation.' They had reached a road edged with guest-houses and small super-markets, and the traffic thickened around them until they were moving slowly in a long line of cars.

Tapping impatiently on the steering-wheel, Dempsey cast a sidelong glance at Philip and was pleased to see some colour in his face and a growing interest as he watched the families with push-chairs, young people in their rainbow-coloured shorts, older couples, their faces shiny with the warmth of the afternoon.

'I think it will be too far to go to Newquay, just for the afternoon, but I thought we could have a look at the surfing on Penhelly sands, walk along the promenade, then have some tea before head-ing back. Do you fancy that?' Dempsey changed down and pulled up at a red traffic-light, then turned to look at Philip.

'Don't mind. I'd rather go up to the cliff path, if it's not too much trouble for you. Blow away a few cobwebs.'

'Of course.' Delighted that Philip had offered a suggestion, Dempsey would have been happy to push the chair up a mountain! It seemed to take nearly that much effort, once they'd found a place to park, got Philip into his chair and started on their walk. The crowds thinned as they climbed a gentle zig-zag, and before long they reached an open area of grassland, near the path at the edge of the cliff.

'Breezy enough for you?' Dempsey laughed as wind, blowing directly from the sea and smelling of salt and seaweed, ruffled Philip's fair hair. 'Let's sit here for a few minutes, shall we?'

Hoping that the relaxed atmosphere might encourage Philip to confide in her, she settled the chair beside a narrow wooden seat and sat quietly; after a little while her patience was rewarded.

'I've been pretty miserable lately, haven't I, Demps?'

'You've every right to get down-hearted at times. You've been so brave since the accident—perhaps too brave.' Dempsey squeezed his hand.

'I think it hit me when Mum and Dad got Steve, my cousin, to come and work on the farm. Made this——' Philip gestured towards his lap '—seem completely final. Made me give up hope.'

'You mustn't give up hope just because you

can't do the job you're used to. There are all sorts of other things you can do.'

'Such as?' Philip said bitterly. 'Make baskets?'

'All sorts.'

'Of course, if the development went through, there might be more opportunities,' he said thoughtfully.

Dempsey felt as though she'd been hit in the stomach, but she made no comment.

'We'll look into all the possibilities, Dr Saville and I,' she told him.

'You like him, don't you, Demps? Like him a lot, I mean.' Philip stared out towards the horizon, his voice so quiet that Dempsey had to strain to hear the words.

'I think he's a very good doctor and I'm sure that between us we'll think of so much for you to do, it'll make you giddy! I'm going to get us an ice-cream.' Jumping hurriedly to her feet, so that Philip wouldn't see the blush that warmed her face at the mention of Bart's name, Dempsey sped along the path towards the small kiosk they'd passed earlier.

She juggled her purse back into her pocket, then, grasping an ice-cream cone in either hand, walked carefully back along the path. But abruptly she halted, frozen like a statue. She couldn't see the wheelchair. Suddenly she heard the sound of its wheels and it came into view, juddering towards the cliff-edge, with Philip's head bouncing above the back like a rubber ball.

'Philip, no!' Dempsey didn't realise the scream she heard was hers. But before she'd run a few steps, there was a call in a familiar voice from a car parked to her right.

'Philip, hold on!' Effortlessly, Bart raced after the chair, seconds only, it seemed to Dempsey, before it reached the edge of the slope, and seized the handle, his knuckles showing white with the strain of stopping it. On legs like jelly, Dempsey ran towards them.

'Philip, what were you doing?' Half crying with relief, she reached forward, then noticed she was still carrying the ices and threw them down on the ground with a gesture of disgust.

'I'm all right, Dempsey, really I am. I was trying to see a curlew I could hear calling, and the next thing I knew, the chair was running away with me and I couldn't stop it.' Philip's face was white, but his voice came out strongly.

'Let's see your hands.' Gently Bart took hold of Philip's wrists and turned his palms face upwards. There were streaks of dirt and deep grazes from the wheels on both. 'We'd better get you somewhere to clean those up, and I think we could all do with a cup of tea.' Bart looked searchingly at Dempsey, but didn't say any more until they reached the kiosk, where he ordered a tray of tea and brought it to their table outside. He ran a finger around the collar of his tan-coloured shirt as he sat down.

'I didn't do it on purpose, truly I didn't.' Philip's head hung down, his face hidden from both Dempsey and Bart.

'I never thought you did,' Dempsey said gently.

She bent forward and kissed his cheek. 'You've always had more than your share of courage.'

'You were quick off the mark.' Philip turned to Bart and managed a shaky grin. 'What I'd call good reflexes.'

'Just lucky to have been in the right place at the right time,' Bart said, biting firmly into a chocolate biscuit.

'How did you happen to be here?' Dempsey asked curiously.

'You said you might be coming here with Philip, and I wanted to see him, so I thought I'd try and find you.'

'Thank heaven you did!' Dempsey said in heartfelt tones, leaning forward and giving Philip a hug.

'Glad to have been of service, but please don't frighten Dempsey or me like that again,' Bart said firmly, tapping Philip on the chest.

'Of course I won't. Anyway, what did you want to see me about?'

'I'll come round this evening, if that's all right? Now if you're sure you're both OK I must make a move. Enjoy the rest of the afternoon.' Draining his cup, Bart set it on the tray and hurried off, leaving a very subdued pair behind him.

'Do you mind if we go home now?' Philip leaned across the table and touched Dempsey's arm. 'I still feel a bit shaky and rather sore.'

'Oh, Philip, I'm sorry, I forgot your poor hands. Let's get back and I'll put some antiseptic on them for you.' She had been lost in thought, her mind on Bart's fortunate appearance, then the way he'd seemed so strained just before he left them. He was certainly a difficult person to understand at times, she mused as she released the brake on the chair and began to push it carefully back to the car.

CHAPTER EIGHT

'DEMPSEY, guess who?' The voice echoed down the wire, making Dempsey blink as she hurriedly tried to pull herself from sleep.

'Er—er—hello?' she mumbled.

'I didn't wake you, did I? I'm terribly sorry. It's David Morgan. I just rang to thank you for doing such a good job on the house. Mary is thrilled to bits.'

'Hello, David. How's Jenny?'

'Improving slowly—that's why we thought we'd take a chance and come home now.' He paused. 'And, of course, it's worked out very well, with Dr Saville having to leave suddenly.'

Dempsey froze.

'Dempsey, are you there?'

'Yes, I'm here. Did you say, Dr Saville leave?' she echoed.

'Oh, sorry, didn't he tell you? Probably there wasn't enough time. He's had a call from his father in New York and has to fly out there as soon as possible.'

'New York?' She tried to force her mind into gear, but her thoughts stumbled as though a cog were missing. 'His father isn't ill, is he?'

'No, it's business.' David laughed. 'You know what these tycoons are like, flying off at the drop of a hat.'

No, I don't know what they're like, Dempsey
thought fiercely. You tell me. How could he go
without even a word of farewell? She cleared her
throat. 'Is he coming back?'

'I'm not sure. He said he'd be pleased to help
again if we have to go back to Cardiff. Anyway, I
must go now—Mary wants a word.'

If anyone had asked Dempsey afterwards what
Mary had said or what her answers had been, she
wouldn't have known. She felt frozen like a fly in
amber. Everything she heard seemed to be reaching her from a distance, and it wasn't until she
was about to hang up that she realised she had
accepted an invitation to the Morgans's for the
following day.

'Oh, Mary, I'm sorry; I've already arranged to
go to Rita's,' she apologised.

'That's all right, I've asked her as well. Just a
thank you for looking after the house.'

'I hope you didn't mind?'

'Mind? What about?' Mary's soft Welsh voice
was puzzled.

'Well, that we did the housework? We guessed
that you wouldn't have had time to organise
anything, leaving in such a rush.'

'I couldn't think of a nicer welcome home.
Anyway, I must go, and I'll look forward to seeing
you tomorrow. About twelve o'clock all right?'

'Yes, fine, thank you, Mary.' Sinking back on to
the cushions of the settee, Dempsey slowly
replaced the receiver. For a moment she gazed
with unseeing eyes through the window. The
evening shone golden with the rays from the

setting sun, outlining the trees. A flock of circling swallows were black dots against the sky as they looked for a resting-place. Swarms of gnats hovered under the branches of a dark green japonica, but Dempsey saw none of it.

Her thoughts were fixed on one thing only— that Bart could have left without contacting her, letting her discover the news second-hand. Wearily she stood, absent-mindedly patting the cushions on the settee back into shape, and stared with amazement at the clock. She'd been asleep for nearly two hours! Pushing her fingers through her hair, she walked towards the kitchen then, with a start, remembered the answering machine.

Almost running to the table, she switched it on and waited as a single message clicked into place.

'Hi there, Miss Dempsey.' Bart's rich, deep voice seemed to fill the room. 'I have to rush off— business problems in New York. I'll send you a postcard. I've enjoyed my time in Penmawtha and I hope we can get together soon. Oh, by the way, could you take the archery set to Philip for me? It'll probably come better from you, anyway.' Dempsey stared at the machine, willing it to tell her more, trying to read some hidden meaning in the few words, but, though she played the tape through until she knew the message by heart, the only feeling apparent was one of pleasant friendliness.

She looked again at the clock before going to the kitchen to make herself a cup of tea. It was too late to go and see Philip now. They'd sat for some time talking after getting back to his bungalow at

the farm and, as Dempsey had cleaned the grazes
on his hands and helped him prepare a drink,
she'd sensed that the events of the afternoon had
acted on Philip in such a way that he was much
calmer and brighter.

Now, as she poured boiling water into a mug
and toasted some bread, her thoughts went back
again to Bart. She hadn't switched on the answering machine on her return, suddenly overcome by
weariness.

'If I had,' she said aloud through a mouthful of
toast, 'I might have had a chance to say goodbye.'

Would that have been wise? an inner voice
asked. Could you have remained calm and
friendly and not betrayed how you felt? And how
do I feel? Dempsey sank back on the settee and
put her feet up on a stool. She switched on the
television, but saw none of the programme, the
flickering screen only a background to her
thoughts.

If she were honest, if she were really honest,
she would have to admit that she had fallen in
love with Bart. The knowledge earlier that he had
left Penmawtha had been like a stab to the heart.
A twisted little smile crossed her face at the cliché,
but it described exactly how she'd felt. As though
someone had plunged a knife into her. Then had
come numbness and a sense of disbelief.

Now that she was facing facts more honestly,
there was a feeling almost of relief, though she
still had an ache deep inside.

'And what good does it do me, knowing how I
feel?' The words drifted towards the ceiling as she

leaned back. 'And more to the point, what good does it do, when Bart obviously doesn't feel the same way? Oh, Dempsey,' she sighed, 'you're an idiot, talking to yourself like this. Come on—bath and bed.'

'Any news?' Rita looked up as Dempsey hurried into the surgery and flung her hat towards the coat-stand.

'Why does it always land on the floor?' Dempsey muttered in exasperated tones as she bent to retrieve it. 'It looks so easy when they do it on the films.'

'Judging by the change of subject,' Rita said drily, 'I assume you haven't heard anything from the other side of the Atlantic?'

'Not a word, Rita.' Suddenly subdued, Dempsey walked behind the desk and rested one hip against the filing cabinet, trying to ignore the sympathy in Rita's eyes.

'Come on; coffee. And a list a mile long. Nothing like hard work for curing the blues.' Rita slapped a piece of paper in front of Dempsey, then filled their two mugs with coffee.

'Rita, you're impossible. But I don't know what I'd do without you.' Dempsey picked up the list of patient visits for the day. Though she tried to put on a brave face, especially at work, the continuing silence from Bart had become a nagging pain. Empty days, despite being busy, led into sleepless nights that were making her usual healthy glow fade like rose petals at the end of summer. Surely he could have sent a postcard?

Even a friendly note would have been better than nothing. But there had been no word since his departure four weeks previously.

She felt drained, unable to concentrate, and found she had to use more and more make-up in an effort to disguise the dark circles under her eyes and add colour to her cheeks.

'You're right about the visits.' Dempsey quickly scanned the list of names. 'This should keep my mind well occupied for the whole day. And into the evening as well, I should think.' She paused. 'Who's this?' She pointed to a name at the bottom.

'Let me see.' Rita pushed her glasses on to her nose. 'Mrs Marston, Ben's mother. She had a nasty reaction to a wasp sting and I said you'd look in to make sure it's all right. Sorry.' Rita lifted her hands in apology at the expression on Dempsey's face.

'I don't mind,' said Dempsey. 'At least she hasn't worried so much about Ben lately.'

'Ever since you arranged those lung-function tests she's been much happier. That was a good idea.'

'Bart thought so too,' Dempsey murmured, trying to control a lurch of pain that knotted at her inside.

'And isn't the news good about Vera?' Rita gabbled on. 'She's been a different person since she started housekeeping at the Morgans's house.'

In spite of herself, Dempsey giggled. 'I still can't picture her on a push-bike, though, can you?'

'Not really, but it's worked out well, particularly

as Mary is still travelling backwards and forwards to Cardiff so often.'

'And there's Philip, with his computer and his archery.' Dempsey refilled the coffee-mugs and perched on the edge of a chair. 'I believe he's driving his father daft with ideas for programmes! He's started one, apparently, that gives the optimum feed to milk production ratio for the cows, so that there's a correct balance between grass and supplementary protein nuts at this time of year.'

'Sounds faintly rude, but I'll believe you.' Rita looked up as the door opened.

'Good grief,' she muttered under her breath, 'the first patient's arrived and I'm still gossiping! I'll have to hurry or Dr Morgan will be here before I'm ready.'

Dempsey took the hint and walked through to her office. She didn't have much to prepare before starting her round, for most of the calls were straightforward. She picked up the list.

'Mrs Bagstock, dry dressing. Mrs Marston, reassurance. Mr Tregarron, glad he's sticking to his diet now. Must be hard for him to give up his beloved pasties, even though it means he doesn't have to have insulin injections.' Concentrating as she read the list, at first Dempsey ignored the buzz of the intercom.

'Yes, Rita, what is it?' she said impatiently.

'Don't snap,' Rita said in a superior tone, 'or I shan't put your call through from New York.'

'What did you say?' Dempsey's voice came out as a whisper and she had to hold tightly to the edge of the desk to stop her hand shaking.

'Hold on—call from New York,' Rita carolled.

'Hello?'

'Dempsey? Is that Miss Dempsey?' As clearly as if he were in the next room, Bart's voice reached her, making her nerves quiver with shock.

'Yes, it's me. Is there something wrong?'

'Now why should you think that?' Dempsey could hear the smile in Bart's voice.

'Well, phoning me now. What's the time there?' Oh, what a stupid question, Dempsey groaned to herself.

'It's three o'clock in the morning here—an ungodly hour, I know—but I thought I'd ring and warn you to get some time off. I've decided to have a birthday party for my thirtieth and I want you to come.'

'And you're phoning me now to ask me?'

'Well, I knew I'd be sure to get you at the surgery and, as I've experienced before, with such a will-o'-the-wisp, I don't know when I'd manage to reach you later in the day. And of course the invitation includes Philip, if he'd like to come.'

'I should think he'd love to,' Dempsey said, surprised at the idea. 'He's doing well with his archery, by the way. Seems much happier and more at peace with himself.'

'Glad to hear it. Anyway, I'm having my party at the beginning of August and I'll be sending you a note with the details as soon as I get back to the UK, hopefully in a couple of days.'

'I'm glad it wasn't bad news that took you to the States.' Dempsey cradled the receiver to her ear as though the contact would somehow bring her closer to Bart.

'No, not bad news. Just some problems with the finance for the development, but Dad and I have ironed out the wrinkles, so it should be plain sailing from now on. Anyway, I'd better get some sleep and let you start work. Take care and, as they say on this side of the pond, "Have a nice day."'

'Goodbye, Bart,' Dempsey murmured, but he'd already hung up and there was only a shrill noise on the line to prove that she hadn't dreamt the call, that it had actually happened.

'Sorry to burst in——' her office door swung open and Rita appeared '—but I'm nearly prostrate with curiosity. It was him, wasn't it?' Rita's smile was wider than a slice of water-melon, almost dividing her face in two.

'Yes, it was, and he rang to ask me to go to his birthday party in August.'

'He—he rang from New York to ask you that?' Rita stuttered in disbelief.

'That's what the man said. Oh, Rita——' Dempsey jumped up and seized her friend by the waist and spun her round, knocking papers from the desk to the floor '—he must like me a little bit, to phone all the way from New York!'

'More money than sense but, if it puts the stars back in your eyes, I'm delighted for you. Now I must dash.'

Rita hurried away as Dempsey sat trying to bring some order to her whirling thoughts. Even the mention of the development wasn't enough to dampen her spirits. We'll sort that out when we get there, she thought, humming to herself as she tried to straighten the desk, which was as chaotic as her thoughts.

'I'm on my way. If I get time, I'm going up to my cottage to see how the repairs are getting on,' she called to Rita as she left the surgery, laughing at her friend's exaggerated wink. She sped through the visits as though on wings.

'Lovely, lovely day,' she sang, steering her little car along the narrow roads. The sky seemed more blue, the sun was brighter, scarlet-headed poppies danced in the cornfields, and a thrush seemed to sing her a personal serenade when she got back in the car after visiting Mrs Bagstock.

'Good morning, Vera.' Dempsey slowed and called from the window as she passed the red-faced, puffing figure on a bicycle.

'Morning, Dempsey. You look well.' Vera waved an uncertain hand before seizing the handlebars again.

'So do you. How's the job going?'

'Proper, thank you. I love it. I don't think I'd want to give it up, even when the development gets going. They're lovely people, the Morgans, aren't they?'

'Certainly are.' Dempsey edged past and drove on. Her cottage was situated at the head of the valley, where a road led down to the harbour. Sometimes she let it out in the summer months to friends, but since its storm damage earlier in the year she had taken the opportunity to get alterations done at the same time as the repairs.

She hadn't been there for several weeks, and guilt at her neglect sent her onward. It wasn't long before she pulled up at the narrow wicket gate. There was no work going on at the present time, but she was delighted to see that the newly thatched roof with the stork insignia of the thatcher was completed, and a glass extension to replace one broken by a falling tree in the winter gales sparkled in the sun's rays.

Unlocking the front door, Dempsey wandered into the sitting-room that opened directly from it, and went to the windows overlooking the valley. It smelt a little musty from lack of use, but there was no sign of damp, for the ceiling had completely dried out.

I ought to get the alterations finished and move back in here, she thought, looking round with a proprietorial air. But the flat was very convenient and much nearer to the surgery. She rubbed at a smudge on the dusty window, then stared hard. A few feet away in her garden stood a man, a complete stranger to her, with a tripod. At first she thought he was taking photographs, but then realised the instrument he was using was a theodolite. He was a surveyor.

Dempsey flung open the window.

'What are you doing?' she demanded.

He jumped visibly. As he turned, Dempsey saw he was holding a clipboard and ruler.

'Nothing to worry about, love,' he called back in a strong London accent. His shirt and jeans were well-worn but looked good quality, and he had a pleasant smile. 'Just doing a survey.'

'What for? I'm not having any work done that needs a survey.'

He pushed his thick grey hair back from his forehead.

'Nothing to do with the cottage, if that's what you mean. It's for the Saville development.'

'You didn't get permission to come on my land,' Dempsey said coldly, 'and I'd like you to leave right now.'

'Just going,' he shrugged, and she caught sight of an estate car at the side of the road; whistling cheerfully, he climbed in and drove off.

What a nerve! she thought, opening the rest of the windows to let the soft summer air blow through the cottage. But even this encounter wasn't enough to spoil her mood, and she was still humming as she finished going through the rooms. Soon she left, locking the front door behind her.

It was only a short drive to the harbour and the site of the proposed development. Perhaps she'd better look round it again. She hadn't thought much about it since Bart's departure, but now it was pushed into the forefront of her mind, partly by Vera's words earlier and also by her meeting with the surveyor.

There were two fishing-boats tied up beside the small breakwater and a boat she hadn't seen before, a launch with an awning that stretched out from a small cabin aft of the mast. It looked expensive, with its highly polished wooden deck and the fresh blue and white paintwork. Parking at the end of the breakwater, Dempsey stared curiously at the boat before leaving the car and wandering towards it. The name wasn't visible at first, but then, as she approached, she could clearly see the distinctive 'S.E.' logo along the gunwale. Another display of the Savilles's wealth, she thought, starting to become a little edgy. There was no one on board, and the two fishing-boats were empty as well. Unable to get any information, Dempsey hurried back to the car and drove away, soon reaching Ted Nancarrow's office. The councillor was there when she arrived, and delighted to see her.

'Morning, Sister, what can I do for you?'

'Have the plans been passed for the development?' Breathlessly, Dempsey asked the question almost before she got through the door.

'Not that I know of. Here, sit down.' He pushed a chair towards her and sat back in his own. 'What makes you think that it might have been? Mind you——' he pulled a face '—with the fishing the way it is, I sometimes wonder if it would be entirely a bad thing.' He picked up a file and scanned several sheets of paper inside, not noticing Dempsey's frown of dismay. Was she the only person whole-heartedly against the leisure centre? Her earlier happiness began to fade as worry about the morning's events crowded in on her.

Quickly she related the news of the surveyor in her garden, the fact that Vera Summers seemed to think it was a fait accompli, that there was a boat in the harbour from the Saville company.

'Well, according to the paperwork——' Ted peered at the file '—everything still has to be decided. But I'll look into it. I should be having a meeting with John Saville—let me see, some time next week.'

Dempsey stood up. 'I'd be very grateful if you'd tell me what the outcome is.'

'You'd be the first to hear, don't worry. After all, your family is more or less responsible for Penmawtha being here.' Getting to his feet, Ted walked around the table and opened the door. 'Thanks for calling in. As I say, I'll look into it.'

Thoughtfully, Dempsey walked along Fore Street, and turned into the post office and village shop. She soon had her few purchases of stamps and airmail letters completed, and walked slowly back to the car. There were still several calls to make, but she found it difficult to concentrate on work. Two voices sounded in her head. One was Bart's: 'You'll be the first to know.' The other was Ted's, saying the same thing. How was it that everything pointed towards the development becoming a possibility? Was she being too sensitive? Angrily she shook her shoulders in denial. She had to trust Bart. She had to. If she had hopes of any sort of relationship in the future, trust was vital.

Hey, she told herself sharply, who mentioned anything other than a friendly invitation? Don't start setting your hopes too high. But she couldn't control a flutter of excitement at the memory of Bart's telephone call.

I'll have to get something new to wear, she thought. She pulled the car round the next corner and braked hurriedly as she reached the Marstons' bungalow. I'll have to go to Plymouth and get an outfit. Stay with Richard and Joanna. I haven't visited them for ages, and Jo's just the person to help me choose.

Dempsey's sister-in-law, a tall, elegant brunette, always made Dempsey feel very much the country cousin, but she would be honest in selecting an outfit that brought out Dempsey's good points—that, Dempsey knew well.

And a present! What can I get Bart, a wealthy jet-setter, who probably has everything he wants or needs? The shopping trip to Plymouth was going to be a headache in more ways than one.

CHAPTER NINE

'HAVE you seen the sunset I've ordered especially for you?' Taking Dempsey by the elbow, Bart led her out through french windows and on to a large paved terrace that ran the length of one side of the house, a house that Dempsey was still trying to find her way around. The sunset that lit up the sky to the west was well worth seeing. A fiery red sky faded as they watched, leaving streaks of cloud that were all the colours of the spectrum, ranging from a delicate rose-pink through crimson to a deep heliotrope behind a tree-covered slope that marked the boundary of the garden.

The Surrey countryside was much gentler than the granite slopes of Dempsey's beloved Cornwall, but still as beautiful in its own way. Not speaking, she watched the changing colours, but was still too bemused by the day's events to really appreciate the beauty of the scene.

Since the arrival of Bart's card, giving her the date of the party and the details of his address, Dempsey had lived in a whirl that had barely stopped spinning right up to the time she had arrived that morning.

Arranging nursing cover for her holiday, then a two-day shopping trip to Plymouth, which left her footsore and more weary than she would have thought possible, hurried arrangements about the flat and the cottage, had made the days rush by.

Possibly it's just as well that I've hardly had time to breathe, she thought, as she strolled with Bart over the gravel of a curving driveway. At least it's stopped my nerve giving way altogether. She glanced up at him; he was unusually silent, his pale grey suit and white shirt almost blending in the dimness of the gathering evening.

She was relieved that she'd had the sense, or rather that she'd followed Joanna's advice, to buy several outfits. Bart and his father maintained a much more formal lifestyle than the one she was used to, and she had to admit that it boosted her confidence, knowing that the softly draped peach-coloured dress she was wearing suited her so well. She'd been warmed by the appreciative light in Bart's eyes at dinner and his father's compliments.

'Is it too cool for you out here?'

'No, I'm fine.' Dempsey smiled in the dusk, for her shiver had nothing to do with the temperature, but was a direct result of Bart's nearness and the way his hand brushed hers as they moved towards the edge of a lawn that looked like black velvet away from the lights of the house.

She turned to look back.

'How long have you lived here?' Seen in the present dim light, a lot of the house's charm wasn't apparent, but when Dempsey had first set eyes on it she had been unable to prevent a gasp of delight.

'We've been here ever since we moved down

from Yorkshire. Of course, when my father bought it, it wasn't as it is now. It hadn't been lived in for years; in fact I think, judging by the state of some of the rooms, it must have been used to keep goats and pigs inside.' He wrinkled his nose. 'I can still remember the smell. But Dad saw the potential straight away, or so he says.' Bart laughed affectionately. 'Anyway, he fell in love with it and here we've been ever since. It's nice, isn't it?'

'Nice?' Dempsey echoed the word incredulously. 'I can't think of a less adequate word to describe it. It's absolutely lovely. And it has a warm—I don't know, a welcoming feel about it——'

'That's because you are welcome,' Bart interrupted, taking her hand and gently kissing it.

'Tell me some of its history.' Breathlessly, she pulled her hand away and moved back towards the light spilling out on to the terrace.

'If you're sure you won't be bored.' Testing the cushions on a wrought-iron seat, Bart sat down. 'Come on——' he patted the seat beside him '—it's not damp, and it's a shame to waste one of the few evenings where it's possible to sit outside.'

Dempsey slowly lowered herself alongside.

'Relax, Dempsey, I'm not going to eat you!'

'I'm fine.' She pulled her skirt around her and looked at him shyly. This wasn't quite what she'd had in mind when she'd asked for the house's history. This romantic setting, with the soft evening air caressing her skin, Bart's deep voice sending shivers down her spine and the heady perfume from a nearby rose-bed, which blended with the aroma of some night-scented stock. As if sensing her wariness, Bart turned away and folded his arms.

'History of the house, part one,' he said, a grin lifting the corner of his mouth. 'There was a house here in Tudor times, but I don't think there's much of that left now. Some of the brickwork and the foundations, over by the garages, are probably from that time. I think the main building behind us dates from the end of the eighteenth, beginning of the nineteenth centuries, but there've been lots of additions over the years.'

Dempsey looked over her shoulder at the wide sash-windows, and recalled the small portico at the front entrance.

'It has a look of Jane Austen about it, doesn't it?'

'I suppose it does,' Bart agreed thoughtfully. 'When you've grown up with a place and lived through some of the alterations, with builders, plumbers, roofers, electricians, carpet-fitters and curtain-makers, and then seen the final results as they are now, the original is difficult to picture. My father is American enough in his ideas to have lots of bathrooms with decent plumbing, and in his Yorkshire good sense makes sure that everything works as it should.'

'Oh, please,' Dempsey sighed, 'you're destroying all my romantic illusions. Plumbing!' She snorted. 'I was picturing ladies in Empire-style dresses and poke-bonnets, strolling in the garden, writing letters, painting water-colours. . .'

'Fluttering their fans as they teased their suitors. Go on.' Bart leaned towards her, his eyes pools of blackness.

'Nothing,' Demspey muttered hastily. 'I love Jane Austen's books, and this seemed a perfect setting, that's all.'

'Oh, I see.' Bart sat quietly for a moment. 'You haven't told me about Philip. How is he now? I rather thought you'd bring him with you.'

Dempsey blinked at the sudden change of subject. 'You'll never believe the difference in him.' Her eyes sparkled. 'He's too busy with his computer to get away, and he's progressing marvellously with his bows and arrows.'

'Do you mean he's becoming an expert toxophilite?' Bart said in a mock-superior tone.

'I mean he's having a wonderful time, learning to use the archery set you gave him, and it's improving his general health, because he's always outside practising; when he isn't reorganising his father's farm with the aid of his computer, that is. And,' Dempsey added, 'the best news of all.' She paused.

'Well, go on, I can hardly wait,' Bart said drily.

'There's a young lady at the computer class, and the name "Amy" seems to feature pretty often in Philip's conversation these days.'

'And you don't mind?' Bart leaned across the seat and took hold of Dempsey's hand.

'Of course not—I'm delighted. As long as she doesn't hurt him.' Trying to ignore the subtle pressure of Bart's fingers on hers, she desperately sought another subject. 'And have I told you about. . .?'

'Dempsey,' Bart whispered, 'please, stop talking for a moment.' Gently he put one hand behind her neck and pulled her towards him. She gazed, mesmerised, as his face came ever closer. His mouth was warm and sweet; the smell and taste of him filled her nostrils, blending in a mixture of sensation that made her head spin. Gently his lips traced a path towards her earlobe, then moved to her neck, planting tiny kisses, every one of which burned her skin like fire.

As if of their own volition, Dempsey's arms moved round behind Bart's neck, her fingers delighting in the springy texture of his hair. A low groan of pleasure came from her throat when his head moved further down towards her breast, his hand pulling aside the neckline of her dress, his mouth pressing delicately on the sensitive rosebud of her nipple. She was lost in a cascade of feeling, which warmed her blood so that all she wanted was for Bart to continue his exploration of her body as his expert caresses roused her to ever greater levels of desire. The night was filled with him, with his masculine fragrance, with the feel of his body pressed against hers.

'Dempsey,' he murmured throatily, 'Dempsey, you're enough to drive any man mad.' Suddenly there was the sound of a door slamming, and Bart stiffened before pulling her upright on the seat.

'Dempsey, I'm sorry, I don't know what came over me. I must have been carried away by the. . .by the. . .' His words were lost in the harsh sound of his breathing; not looking at her, he leaned forward and rested his elbows in his knees, his head in his hands.

'Are you all right?' he muttered, but she could barely hear him. Her whole body was trembling, like an over-tuned violin that had been tossed to the ground.

'What's the matter, Bart?' Even to her own ears, her voice sounded strained.

'I'm a fine host!' He laughed harshly. '"Come and look at the garden, and on the way back we'll have a quick seduction, all part and parcel of the tour."' Impatiently, he pushed back a lock of hair from his forehead, staring straight ahead, his hands white-knuckled on the edge of the seat.

Slowly he turned towards her and cupped her face in his hands. 'You'd better go inside, Dempsey.' Gently he kissed the end of her nose. 'I can only apologise and say that I shall make sure I don't behave like that again.'

But I want you to, her senses cried, though none of her feelings showed on her face. Confused and upset, she picked up her bag and went into the house.

'There you are, my dear.' Mr Saville's voice came from a deep button-backed armchair as Dempsey walked through the comfortable pink and green furnished drawing-room. 'Are you off to bed, or would you like a nightcap?'

'I'd like a small brandy, please.' Defiantly, she perched on a stool beside John Saville's chair. She wasn't about to reveal to him or his son how agitated she was feeling, by rushing off to bed like some teenager. Mr Saville went to a rosewood sideboard, took out two brandy snifters and poured a measure into each one.

'I think I'll join you, as Bart doesn't seem to be around to take care of you. Are you quite sure you're happy with this?' He passed her a glass. 'I can easily get hot milk or some such thing organised, if you'd rather.'

'This is lovely.' Gently Dempsey swirled the tawny liquid and sniffed at it deeply before taking a sip. She didn't usually drink anything stronger than a glass of wine, but the fiery spirit seemed ideal to try to disperse some of the tension she felt, and it filled her with a glow that was nearly as warming as Bart's kisses.

'Has Bart been looking after you?' Mr Saville looked at her over the rim of his glass and swallowed. There was something so reminiscent of Bart in the gesture that Dempsey felt a lump come into her throat. When she'd first arrived at the house, she had been in awe of John Saville, or at least all that he stood for. But he had gone out of his way to make her feel at home, and the strong physical likeness between him and his son, their obvious affection for one another, had dispelled her shyness, and now she felt at ease with him as they sipped their drinks.

'He's been taking very good care of me,' she answered, unaware of the wry expression that crossed her face as she spoke.

'Possibly I shouldn't tell you this, but he's very fond of you.' Mr Saville cleared his throat. 'He's had relationships in the past. I hope I'm not speaking out of turn when I say it, but I don't remember his having such a marked affection for someone for a long time. So I hope any differences regarding the development won't alter how you feel towards him.'

Dempsey couldn't think how to reply. Every word spoken by Bart's father burned into her brain. Was he trying to tell her that his son felt only friendship for her? Was he warning her away from any emotional involvement with Bart? And if Bart did feel only friendship for her, which was what she'd thought prior to this evening, why had he been so aroused by their lovemaking? For every womanly instinct she possessed knew that Bart was as stirred as she was during those few minutes they had spent on the terrace.

'I'm very fond of Bart, Mr Saville.' She managed a laugh. 'Development or no development, I'm sure we're both adult enough to be able to cope with such differences.' But not with how I feel whenever he's near me or touches me or kisses me, her inner self screamed silently.

'I know you are.' Slowly Mr Saville drained his glass and rose from the chair. Even the way he moves is like Bart, Dempsey thought, watching him as he went towards the door.

'I'm off to bed, if you'll excuse me. I find it takes longer for me to recover from jet lag these days.' He paused in the doorway. 'Are you sure there's nothing else I can get you? I don't know what's happened to that son of mine. He's not being a very good host at the moment.'

'I think he wanted to spend more time in the

garden. I'll get an early night myself; must get my beauty sleep for the big day.' Dempsey smothered a yawn. 'What's the programme for tomorrow, Mr Saville?'

'I'm leaving it all to Bart. The guests are arriving at about eight o'clock, and that's all I know.' He bent and kissed her cheek. 'Goodnight, lass. Sleep well.'

Dempsey hurried past him in the doorway. Suddenly she couldn't face the thought of seeing Bart again that night, and the idea of a leisurely bath and an early night with a good book had an overpowering attraction. She ran lightly up the polished wood staircase, turning on to a long landing that stretched along the house, dark-painted doors opening on either side. Her bedroom was at the far end, and she quickly slipped inside, calling a final goodnight to John Saville as she did so.

Dempsey paused. Her earlier impression came back to her with renewed force. Like the rest of the house, this was a lovely room. A double bed, covered by a white duvet, faced an enormous wardrobe with smoked-glass doors. An antique polished desk stood in one corner, and the deep rose velvet of a chaise-longue matched the colour of the carpet.

Swiftly she switched on the bedside light and walked over to the window. Pulling back the edge of the curtain, she gazed out at the garden. From the corner, she could just see the end of the terrace, and her breath caught in her throat at the sight of Bart still sitting where she had left him earlier.

The urge to run down to him was almost overwhelming, and she stood for a long moment, watching the play of light on his dark hair and his easy grace as he sat, lost in thought, even in his stillness giving the impression of controlled power. Suddenly he looked up, and Dempsey dropped the curtain hastily into place, not wanting to be caught staring at him. Her heart beating rapidly, she went into the adjoining bathroom and turned on the taps. Her reflection as she creamed off her make-up gave no sign of the turmoil she had felt ever since she'd been in Bart's arms. Just a shadow in the depths of her eyes hinted at it. And heaven help her, she didn't know what she was going to do, for she had no idea if Bart returned her love. And there was no doubt about it—a one-way love could be a recipe for heartbreak.

'Good morning.' Dempsey stared in surprise at the middle-aged woman who had spoken. She was carrying a tray, which she balanced expertly on one hip as she pulled a small table beside the bed. Dazed with sleep, Dempsey scrambled up against the pillows.

'I didn't expect this,' she protested. 'What time is it? I'm usually up and about really early.'

'It's only eight o'clock, but Dr Saville suggested we give you a call. He said something about wanting to leave soon, and thought you might like to go with him.'

'Go? Where, Mrs—er——?'

'He didn't say, and it's Mrs Culhane.'

'I'd better get moving.' Hastily Dempsey pushed aside the duvet and swung her legs out over the edge of the bed.

'You've got plenty of time. Get back and enjoy your breakfast. Dr Saville isn't in that much of a hurry.' Mrs Culhane's thick black hair was tied back in a bow, the same bright blue as her crisp overall. She was as bright and perky as a robin, bustling round the room, and Dempsey felt almost decadent in contrast.

'I'm a sort of housekeeper, I suppose you'd call it.' Mrs Culhane flicked the curtains tidily into line, letting in the sunshine of what promised to be a lovely morning. 'I run the house and look after the Savilles.'

'Have you been with them long?' Carefully Dempsey straightened the tray on her lap and sipped fresh orange juice.

'Nearly twenty years, I should think.' She paused thoughtfully, looking up at the ceiling.

'Then you must have known Bart——'

'I'm sorry, I have to run along—there are a million things to do for this evening. You have your coffee and croissants and we'll have a chat later.'

Mrs Culhane disappeared through the door, and Dempsey started to eat. But she lacked her usual healthy appetite, and after a gulp at the coffee, which was excellent, she jumped out of bed and hurried over to the window. There was a sound of footsteps crunching on the gravel and, as she watched, Bart came into view around the corner of the house. Before she could move out of sight, he had glanced up.

'Good morning, sleepyhead.' He was dressed in a white shirt and tan trousers, his suede jacket slung over one shoulder. He looked cool and fresh and wide awake, his teeth gleaming as he grinned in a friendly fashion.

'You have me at a disadvantage,' Dempsey called, such a glow of love sweeping through her that she couldn't understand why it wasn't emblazoned on her forehead in letters of flame.

'That's a leading statement. Hurry up and get dressed; I'm going to take you out for the day.'

'Where are we going?' She asked breathlessly.

'Surprise. Wear comfortable walking shoes.'

It didn't take Dempsey long to obey Bart's instructions. Within minutes, she was dressed in a light blue cotton jump suit and white flat-heeled shoes. Seizing a large white handbag, she hurried down the stairs and went outside into the sunshine.

'Sorry to keep you waiting.'

Bart spun round at her words. 'I must say, you have an attribute not common to most women. You certainly can get yourself ready in a very short time.'

'That's a sexist remark if ever I heard one,' Dempsey snorted. 'It's not true at all that women spend hours primping in front of the mirror. It might have been so years ago, but today's working woman hasn't the time to——'

'Whoa! I was only making conversation.' Bart

threw his hands up in front of him in a gesture of submission. 'Subject closed, OK?' He took her elbow and led her towards garages at the far end of the curving gravel drive.

'Dad has to go to the office this morning and will give us a lift.' They clambered into the back of a waiting dark green Bentley behind Mr Saville, who was in the driving seat.

'Morning, Dempsey.' He smiled at her through the rear-view mirror, and soon they were gliding through the tall wooden gates that swung back automatically against brick pillars.

'What have you got planned for the day?' Skilfully, Bart's father manoeuvred the limousine into the passing traffic that was already a thick, continuous stream pouring into the capital.

'It's a surprise. I'll tell you about it this evening.' Mischievously Bart winked at Dempsey, but she was concentrating on the scene outside.

'I'd hate to have to face this every morning.' She looked in horror at the cars cutting and thrusting impatiently.

'You can get used to anything,' Bart grinned.

Despite the heavy traffic, they soon arrived at the Saville offices, in a Georgian terrace near Belgravia where the crisp magnolia paintwork contrasted with shiny black doors and brass fittings.

'It's lovely,' Dempsey said admiringly. 'I expected some multi-storey monstrosity.'

'We're not complete Philistines!' Bart laughed at her expression of apology. 'Come on; it's travel with the rest of the tourists now.' They waved a

farewell to Mr Saville, as he hurried up the steps
and disappeared inside.

Almost running to keep up, Dempsey followed
Bart through the Hyde Park underpass to the
Underground. Jostled by the hurrying passers-by,
she found herself dropping behind. Suddenly he
paused and turned.

'Sorry, I forgot you're not used to the push and
shove of the London crowds.' Firmly he tucked
her arm beneath his own, and the contact lifted
her spirits as they bought tickets and hurried
down the escalator to the train. Nor did he release
his hold. As the train became more crowded, he
took her hand instead, and it was with hands still
linked that they alighted at their station and went
up to street level.

'Where are we going? Am I allowed to ask?'
Smiling at the secretive expression on Bart's face,
Dempsey would have been content to follow him
to the ends of the earth, but she couldn't say that.

'Do you fancy some history?' He looked down
at her. 'My old medical school. And there's
method in my madness—truly.' His smile is
almost irresistible, she thought dreamily.

He'd made no reference to the previous evening
and Dempsey was content to pretend it hadn't
taken place. If they had both been carried away by
the night and the scents of the garden—well, time
would show soon enough what was to happen.
She followed Bart through a narrow courtyard to
a brick building, that when they went inside she
saw was white-tiled and smelt faintly of disinfec-
tant. Passing through double doors, they reached

a hall, where large galleries opened from an iron staircase that spiralled its way up to the centre of the domed ceiling. On one side, shelves held numerous leather-bound volumes, some of them cracked and shabby, and there were glass cases with selections of old-fashioned different-coloured bottles, the fronts of which had Latin names.

'Have you been here before?' Bart smiled at Dempsey's slow shake of her head.

'There's quite a comprehensive history of medicine here, too much to see in one morning, but I thought that some of the progress made over the last hundred years might interest you.'

Still Dempsey didn't fully understand Bart's reasons, but she was soon drawn into studying the various exhibits for their own sakes, and strolled happily, pointing out different items that caught her eye.

'Ugh!' she groaned, then hastily covered her mouth as a lecturer on the floor below looked up.

'What is it?' Bart moved alongside, resting his hand lightly on her shoulder.

'Leeches. I couldn't bear to have one of those on me. Aunt Jess said they sometimes used them even in her day.'

'They use them nowadays, in ophthalmology and, occasionally, in cases of microsurgery.'

'Give me penicillin and the good old hypodermic,' Dempsey shuddered.

'Aha!' Bart said triumphantly. 'So progress need not necessarily be a bad thing.'

'Of course not, but it depends on what you define as progress. Look at this. "Cupping and blistering",' she read. '"Venesection". I saw that done once—on someone with polycythaemia, I think.'

'Rather like blood transfusion in reverse.' For the next hour they studied the glass cases and contents, Dempsey avidly reading the texts.

'Look at this old-fashioned anaesthetic mask, with the gauze and ether that they poured on.'

'Mm—much gentler now, isn't it, with a premed and a tiny intravenous injection.'

'Certainly is, Doctor.' She laughed up at him and found him staring at her in such a way that her breath caught in her throat.

'You should see your face,' he told her.

'Why, what's the matter with it?' Anxiously Dempsey rubbed at her nose.

'It's lovely,' he whispered against her ear.

'Come along, where next?' she said severely.

'Have you had enough yet?'

'No, but if you want to go, I'm quite happy to make a move.'

They went outside, past students sitting on the grass, white-coated figures striding out, full of self-importance, two chattering student nurses, their white shoes twinkling as they hurried along the path.

'I've never seen you in a white coat,' Dempsey observed as they walked slowly in the sunshine.

'But I've seen you in your so efficient-looking navy uniform. Terrifying it is, too.'

'Oh, Bart, what rubbish! I wouldn't frighten anyone.' Dempsey giggled in delight, never having seen Bart in this light-hearted mood before. 'You're in a good mood.'

'Well, what's to be grumpy about?' He shrugged his shoulders and raised his eyebrows, then, taking her by surprise, seized her in a hug that lifted her from her feet.

'Bart!' Dempsey squealed protestingly, but secretly she loved the strength of him holding her.

And his mood lasted throughout the remainder of the day. They walked in Hyde Park, talking non-stop. They laughed over their lunch, Dempsey losing as much spaghetti from her fork as she managed to eat, they rode around London on an open-topped bus, seeing the usual tourist attractions and many secret places that the guide pointed out to them. By the time they arrived back at the Saville office and waited outside for Bart's father to arrive, Dempsey felt about three feet above the ground.

'Thank you for a lovely day.' Daringly, she stretched up and kissed Bart on the cheek.

'My pleasure. But the day hasn't finished yet. We've still got the party this evening.'

'I don't know if I'll last.' She gazed at him wide-eyed, but she knew she could go on for ever, for her blood seemed to fizz in her veins like champagne. And the fizzing sensation didn't desert her during the evening.

The day must have been enchanted. Even Dempsey's make-up after her leisurely bath glided on. Her eyes looked huge as she applied coral and gold shadow, her lips were full and tremulous under the soft layer of lip-gloss and the highlights in her hair glowed copper beneath the bedroom lamp.

'Let's hope your taste is good, Joanna,' Dempsey murmured as she took her dress from the hanger.

The soft gold silk clung deceptively, emphasising every line of her body, with a split in the skirt that showed a flash of leg with each step she took.

'You've got great legs, Dempsey,' her sister-in-law had said. 'Why not show them off?' Wearing high-heeled gold sandals and Joanna's best antique earrings, Dempsey barely recognized the person looking back at her from the mirror.

It's like a scene in a film, she thought, slowly edging into the crowd downstairs. The men in evening dress, the women in all colours of the rainbow, milled and circled from room to room, and suddenly all Dempsey's confidence of earlier in the day vanished like a puff of smoke. Clutching her bag, she sidled past the other guests and made her way to the kitchen.

'Did you want something, Miss Prowse?' Mrs Culhane, with what seemed an army of helpers, was obviously not pleased at having a guest hovering when she was so busy, though she was too polite to say it.

With a nervous grin, Dempsey seized a glass of champagne from a waiter disappearing through the swing door, drained it and followed behind him, blinking at the noise that came from the drawing-room.

'Dempsey, where have you been?' The familiar beloved voice made her spin on her heels and, to his obvious surprise, Dempsey seized Bart in a hug of relief.

'I've been looking for you.' He pushed her away and stared at her for a moment without speaking. 'You look fantastic.'

'So do you.' Dempsey gave a shaky laugh. He was wearing a white dinner-jacket, the light colour a frame for his tanned face. A crimson bow-tie and a handkerchief in his top pocket were the only touches of colour against the black and white of his suit.

'Have you had a drink? You have? Come on, then, let me introduce you to a few people. Ah, here's Dad and Paula, an old friend of his—we'll start with them and then move on to some of the guests.'

With Bart at her side, his hand supporting her elbow, Dempsey smiled and nodded, shook hands and murmured acknowledgement of the various introductions. Gradually she relaxed, helped by another glass of champagne, which she had the sense to drink more slowly than the first.

The rest of the evening printed itself on her memory like a kaleidoscope of whirling impressions, faces, voices, colours, perfumes, with Bart as the hub of the wheel, always there when she needed him, whisking her off to dance, making sure she wasn't left alone, escorting her to the buffet table. Long before she was ready for the party to end, people were collecting coats, saying their goodbyes, and the silence of the night was punctured by the purr of expensive car engines pulling away from the Savilles' house.

'I must admit, now that everyone's gone, I'm whacked.' Dempsey kicked off her sandals and curled up in a big armchair in the drawing-room, which, thanks to Mrs Culhane's efforts, now showed very little evidence of the evening's activities.

'Well, you don't look it. What it is to be young, eh, Paula?' John Saville grinned at the woman beside him. Tall and elegant in black, with greying hair pulled back in a chignon, Paula had gone out of her way to make Dempsey feel at home during the party. 'What about you, Bart?'

His son didn't reply, remaining deep in thought.

'I said what about you—are you "whacked", as Dempsey put it?'

'Not really.' He looked at the others in turn. 'How about a brandy before we all head for bed?'

Both Paula and John Saville shook their heads as one.

'Not for me—I'm off. Come on, Paula, we'll leave these young ones to it. I'll see you to your room.' He took her hand and pulled her up, and they left arm in arm, leaving Dempsey and Bart sitting in silence.

'Well, how about that brandy?' Bart got to his feet and walked over to the sideboard.

'Not for me. I'll get to bed as well.' Suddenly Dempsey felt as flat as the dregs of champagne at the bottom of a glass.

'If not brandy, could you face a breath of fresh air, or are your feet exhausted from dancing the night away?'

'I'd love that.' Dempsey scrambled into her sandals and followed Bart through the french windows to the terrace outside. The air was still warm, and for a minute they stood looking up at the deep velvet of the night sky, stitched with a million stars.

'It's so clear it's almost like the tropics,' Bart murmured. 'I'm not sure if we're about to have our first frost of the year, or if, conversely, it's the greenhouse effect moving our climate south, as it were.'

Gently he put his arm around Dempsey's waist and ushered her away from the lighted windows. 'Come on, Miss Dempsey, I want to talk to you.'

Her heart beating fast, Dempsey walked beside him, trying not to limp in the dainty sandals as they reached the uneven surface of the gravel drive.

She was startled enough to give a small yelp of surprise when Bart swung her up in his arms. 'You can't walk properly in those shoes; I'll carry you,' he announced.

'Where are we going?' Nervously, Dempsey strained against the constricting pressure of Bart's arms, but then the feel of him so close to her, their hearts beating in unison—or was hers particularly loud?—stopped her protestations.

'Here we are.' Bart set her down carefully, beside a small pergola that shone white even in the dimness of the stars' feeble light. 'Are you cold?' For Dempsey shivered.

'No, I'm fine.' What did he want to say to her, that they had to move away from the house?

'Here, take this.' He slipped off his white dinner-jacket and tucked it around her shoulders. She snuggled into its warmth, delighting in the aroma that was Bart—a combination of his after-shave and masculine fragrance.

'This all looks ominous.' Dempsey gave a nervous giggle that was cut off abruptly by Bart's mouth on hers. But the kiss was gentle, the touch as light as a butterfly's wing, and he turned her to face him.

'Can I ask you something personal?'

Dempsey gulped, then nodded.

'You like me, don't you?' She nodded again, her brain racing. More than that, she thought, much more than that.

'Would you consider marrying me?'

With shaking hands, Dempsey reached behind her, feeling for a seat that wasn't there. For a moment she swayed.

'What did you say?' she croaked.

'I didn't expect to have this effect.' Even in the gloom, Dempsey could see the twist of Bart's mouth. 'Sorry if I embarrassed you. It was a silly idea anyway.' He turned and started to walk away.

'Bart, just a minute—give a girl a chance. You can't come out with something like that, with no warning, and expect me to behave as though you'd passed the time of day. It may sound like a stupid question, but why do you want to marry me?'

He swung round to face her.

'Lots of reasons, Miss Dempsey. I'm now thirty

and should be settling down. You're funny, bright, fun to be with, lovely to look at. . .' he paused and walked to her side '. . .and you have a lovely mouth,' he whispered, tracing the outline of her lower lip with his finger.

Dempsey stood, not speaking. Not 'I love you and can't imagine life without you', she thought ruefully. Could she cope with half a loaf? To have Bart as a husband, although he didn't love her?'

'And another reason——' he interrupted her thoughts '—I can't spend much more time in your company without wanting to make love to you, and I like you too much to treat you as just a one-night stand. That's why I brought you all the way out here.' He laughed. 'It's too damned uncomfortable to do anything!'

Dempsey bent and touched the dew-damp grass. 'I don't know,' she murmured.

'Well, don't keep me in suspense; what's the answer?' For the first time since she'd met him, Bart sounded unsure.

'I'd love to marry you, Bart.' She stretched up and kissed him full on the mouth, and felt rather than heard his sigh of relief.

I've got enough love for the two of us, just for starters, she thought, as they turned and walked towards the house, and who knows what tomorrow will bring?

CHAPTER TEN

'GOOD morning.' Nervously, Rita held out a cup of coffee towards her friend, tutting in sympathy at her pale face and set expression. 'Not feeling any better yet, Dempsey?'

Dempsey shook her head. 'Many calls this morning?'

The surgery had been unusually quiet since Dempsey's return from Surrey, but she saw that today's list was quite impressive. 'Good,' she said shortly, 'busy, just how I like it. Is there anyone else outstanding? I might as well complete any backlog.'

'That's the lot so far.' Looking over the rim of her mug, Rita swallowed, then spoke in a rush. 'Dempsey, I don't want to pry, but——'.

'Then don't,' Dempsey said shortly. 'There's nothing to discuss. I'll get my bag and be on my way.'

'You might have to plan your route carefully this morning; there are reports of traffic hold-ups the whole length of the A30.'

Putting her cup down, Dempsey nodded as she walked swiftly to her office and went inside, shutting the door firmly behind her.

I know you mean well, Rita, she thought, but I can't talk about him, I can't. Leaning her head for a moment against the cool wood of the door, her mind travelled back over the previous two weeks. Had the conversation she'd overheard between Bart and his father taken place, or was it some hideous nightmare?

She'd been too excited to sleep the morning after Bart's proposal and, dressed in a swimsuit, had crept downstairs towards the swimming-pool at the back of the house. The sound of voices from John Saville's study had made her dart at first into a nearby doorway. Then, as she'd heard Bart's voice, she had hurried to the study door. But she'd paused unbelievingly at his words.

'I can't imagine that Dempsey will stand in the way of demolishing her cottage, especially when she sees how it will make the development less intrusive.'

Demolish her cottage? She had gasped.

'If I give her something else in its place as a wedding-present, I'm sure she'll come round to our way of thinking.' Despite the thickness of the door, Dempsey had heard every word that John Saville said next.

'It's a good thing you're marrying her. You should be able to persuade her to do what's best for the development, once she's your wife.' The next part of the conversation had dropped to a murmur, then there was a laugh from Bart.

'Why do you think I want to marry her? But she mustn't know anything about it—not yet anyway.'

She had raced back upstairs and thrown her clothes into her suitcase. Searching through her bag, she'd found a scrap of card and had scribbled a few words. She had to get away. How she would open the automatic gates, she didn't know, but she had to flee before she saw Bart or his father, before Bart could see how he'd broken her heart. Frantically, she'd put on a T-shirt, pulled up the zip on her jeans, cursing quietly as she snapped a fingernail, then tiptoed out through the back door. Luck had been with her. The gates were already open for a delivery van, and she had run across the grass to her car, flung her case in the back and driven off without seeing anyone but the delivery driver.

The journey from the Savilles' to her home had seemed endless, not helped by the heavy traffic, which took all her concentration. The motorway had unrolled in front of her like a never-ending black ribbon. She'd driven non-stop as far as Exeter, when exhaustion had made her pull into the services, where she drank a hasty cup of coffee and ate a sticky bun before setting out again. Never had the sight of Penmawtha been more welcome. And never had her determination to keep it as it was been stronger.

Now she must pull herself together and get on with her life. She took a deep breath, tipped her hat down over her eyes, picked up her bag and walked through to the main door.

'Sorry if I snapped,' she said quietly as she passed the desk, but she wasn't sure if Rita heard her apology.

In tune with her mood, banks of lowering cloud filled the sky, but somehow the greyness was easier to bear than a brilliantly sunny day would have been. Flocks of seagulls mewed impatiently as they searched for scraps along the seashore and the adjoining cliffs. The coast road was almost deserted, and Dempsey swung the little car through the bends, trying not to remember the times she had driven the same route with Bart.

To think I admired his honesty in not saying he loved me, she thought, her face rigid with distress. And the proposal was to make sure I didn't stand in the way of the development. When he said he'd do anything for his father, he wasn't joking. Thank God I didn't tell him how I felt. At least I've kept my self-respect there.

She pulled up outside Mrs Bagstock's cottage and hurried up the path. The stormy sky was even more threatening, and she hadn't brought a coat or umbrella. Through the increasing sound of the wind, there was a sudden clatter overhead, and a helicopter appeared, its heavy nose dipping down towards the village as it circled, then moved away.

With a shrug, Dempsey opened the door to Bal Cottage and went inside. For a moment, the noise of voices that greeted her made her blink. In the old-fashioned kitchen, Mrs Bagstock seemed to be submerged in people.

'I'm sorry. . .' Dempsey paused '. . .I didn't know you had visitors. I'll call back later.'

'That's all right, Sister. My family is here for a few days. We can easily go into the bedroom for my dressing.' Slowly the old lady struggled from the chair and limped into the small back bedroom.

'They've all come down for my eightieth birthday.' Proudly Mrs Bagstock waved an arm in the

direction of the kitchen as she sat on the edge of
the bed and rolled down her stocking.

'I didn't realise it was today,' said Dempsey.
'Happy birthday.'

'Actually, it was a couple of days ago, but my
sons and their families couldn't get here before.'

'That looks much better,' Dempsey commented,
looking at the area of pink new skin before she
applied a clean dressing.

'It's since Dr Saville brought me that special
lotion.' Grunting with effort, Mrs Bagstock stood
and balanced a moment against the foot of the bed
before going into the big noisy kitchen.

With a fixed smile covering the wrench she'd
felt at the mention of Bart's name, Dempsey bade
a cheery goodbye, narrowly avoiding two small
boys who were arguing in the garden, and went
to her car.

For a moment she gazed unseeing through the
windscreen. She would have to be stronger than
this. If the mention of Bart's name still brought
such a churning to her inside, it was going to take
ages to forget him.

She looked again at the list and sighed. Mrs
Marston would like a visit. Ben hadn't been well
for the past two days.

'Why doesn't she ever bring him to the surgery?' Dempsey said aloud, then pulled away
hurriedly as she realised Mrs Bagstock's great-
grandsons were watching her one-sided conversation with open mouths.

'Well, no problems with those,' Dempsey muttered after her next visits, the first to a patient

who had just come out of hospital after removal of her gall-bladder. The wound had been very clean.

'Don't forget, a very low fat diet,' Dempsey called through the window of her car, as Mrs Baker shuffled outside with her. The next call, to do a bed-bath, was soon completed.

'Put your arms around my neck,' Dempsey instructed as she swung round, expertly lowering the elderly man into an armchair.

'I don't know how a slip of a thing like you manages to lift someone my size.'

'It's all in the knowing,' Dempsey reassured him, trying not to show the effort she'd made. She tidied her uniform, then drove to the surgery to collect a diet sheet for Mr Tregarron.

Bet he threw the other one away, she thought, the trace of a smile touching her mouth.

'Everything all right?' Rita looked up as Dempsey appeared, and she felt a swift pang of compunction at her friend's wary expression.

'I'm sorry I was such a pig this morning,' she apologised.

'Don't be silly, of course you weren't. Well, actually. . .' Rita paused '. . .I suppose you were, but I'm sure there was a good reason.'

'Even with the best reason in the world, I shouldn't take it out on you,' said Dempsey.

'Don't be daft. That's what friends are for. Oh, by the way, I've had another call from Mrs Marston.'

'I'll go as soon as I've picked up a few bits and pieces.'

'Er—there was also a personal call for you. From Bart.' Rita gabbled the words.

'I've got nothing to say to him. If he rings again, would you tell him I'm out? Have you got a diabetic diet sheet there, please?'

'Of course.' Rita bent down behind the desk and reappeared with the paper in her hand.

'Oh, Dempsey, can you spare a minute?' David Morgan called out to her from his office doorway. 'Come in and sit down.' He pulled a chair forward and perched in his usual fashion on the edge of his desk. 'I don't want to poke my nose in where it's not wanted, but is there anything the matter?' He frowned sympathetically.

Dempsey stared at the floor. And she thought she was doing a good job of disguising how she felt!

'There's not been any problem with my work, has there?' she queried.

'No, of course not. But Mary and I are concerned. You didn't take your full holiday, and you've looked very pale since you got back. I just wanted to make sure that you're feeling all right.' Dr Morgan laughed and patted her hand. 'Can't have my third favourite girl going sick on me, now can I?'

'I'm fine, truly.'

'Well, if you're sure.' He stood up. 'We might be able to bring Jenny home for a long weekend soon. They're very pleased with her progress at the spinal unit.'

'That's wonderful news!' Dempsey paused. 'If there's nothing else?' She hurried out. They were all well-meaning, but the only answer was work and more work to send her to bed exhausted, to keep her mind occupied during the day.

She posted the diet sheet at Mr Tregarron's house, then drove the few miles to the Marstons' bungalow.

She was surprised that no one waited at the door. Usually when Mrs Marston was expecting a visit from Dr Morgan or herself, she had the door open as soon as the car drew up.

Impatiently, Dempsey rang the bell, then rang again. Surely there was someone there?

'Sister, I'm sorry to keep you. I didn't hear you arrive.'

'That's all right. What's the problem, Mrs Marston?'

'Ben seems to have a temperature, so I thought I'd better keep him in bed until you got here. Is Dr Morgan coming?'

'I'll see how Ben is first, shall I?' Without waiting for an answer, Dempsey went into the brightly painted bedroom, where Ben was covered by a duvet, despite the sticky warmth of the morning.

'Let's have a look at you, Ben.' She pulled back the cover and barely prevented a gasp as she saw her patient.

He lay curled up on one side, his face towards the wall. Wheezing breaths struggled from the small body, and his skin was hot and dry to Dempsey's touch.

'How long has he been like this, Mrs Marston?' Quickly Dempsey pulled a thermometer from her bag and tucked it under Ben's arm. 'Ben, have you got any pain?' The little boy whimpered, but still kept his eyes tightly shut.

'How long has Ben been sick?' repeated Dempsey.

'Well. . .' Mrs Marston sat heavily on a stool and pondered for a moment '. . .he hasn't actually been sick. He complained of a headache yesterday, then last night he said his legs were uncomfortable. This morning he wasn't breathing very well, and when I tried to sit him up he screamed as I moved his head forward.'

'Mrs Marston——' Dempsey took her hand '—I think we ought to get Ben to hospital straight away. I'll get Dr Morgan to come and see him. Can I use the telephone?'

'It's through here. What's wrong with him, Sister?' Mrs Marston asked anxiously, her eyes wide.

'I'm not really sure,' Dempsey prevaricated. 'He's very poorly.'

'Oh, Rita, is Dr Morgan there?' To Dempsey's relief, the phone was answered at the first ring. She put her hand over the mouthpiece and turned to Mrs Marston, who was hovering beside her. 'Could you possibly get me a drink, do you think?'

Doubtfully, Ben's mother disappeared in the direction of the kitchen.

'Right, Rita——' Dempsey spoke quietly into the telephone '—get Dr Morgan out to the Marston house as soon as you possibly can. I think Ben might have meningitis, but I don't want his mother to hear what I'm saying, so if I stop talking suddenly you'll know why.'

'Meningitis?' Rita's horror echoed over the wire. 'But Dr Morgan has just gone out on another call; I don't know when he'll be back.'

'In that case, I'd better organise an ambulance without waiting for him.' Dempsey heard the kitchen door open behind her. 'Rita, will you stay at the end of the phone in case I need you? Thanks.'

'I tell you who is here——' Rita began, but Dempsey had replaced the receiver.

'Come and sit down.' Gently she led Mrs Marston into the sitting-room. 'I can't get hold of Dr Morgan at the moment, so I think we'd better get Ben to hospital.'

'Oh, Sister, what's the matter with him? Is it that serious?' Mrs Marston started to cry.

'Now, please get Ben's toilet bag and pyjamas packed while I call an ambulance.' Without waiting to see if Ben's mother did as she'd asked, Dempsey flicked through the pages of her notebook and found the number she wanted. Quickly she described the situation, and sat back with a sigh of relief when the control officer promised an ambulance as soon as possible.

'This is my number.' Dempsey read the digits from Mrs Marston's telephone, hung up, then drank thirstily at the now cold cup of coffee.

I wonder if I should tepid-sponge him? she pondered, going back into the bedroom and looking at the little boy once more. He was still burning hot, and she went into the bathroom and collected a bowl of lukewarm water.

'I'm just getting some water to cool Ben down,'

she called, but Ben's mother couldn't have heard, for there was no reply.

Dempsey stripped off Ben's pyjamas, carefully rolled a towel underneath and began sponging him with long sweeping strokes.

'I feel so helpless,' she moaned to herself. He didn't stir as she began again, even when she added more cold water.

'Ben—Ben! Can you hear me?' Dempsey put her mouth close to his ear, but there wasn't a flicker of response.

'Where's that ambulance?' Demspey didn't realise she had spoken aloud until a startled whisper came from behind her.

'What are you doing, Sister?'

'I'm trying to reduce Ben's temperature. Would you carry on with this while I go and ring to see what's happened to the ambulance?'

But as Dempsey went to pick up the phone it rang under her hand.

'Ambulance control—we're having problems, Sister. There's been a three-car pile-up on the main road, and traffic's backed up for about five miles. We're trying to get through, but, as you can imagine, it's pretty chaotic.'

'I'll have to try and get him there myself.' Quickly Dempsey slammed down the receiver and dialled the surgery number with a hand that was shaking. 'Is Dr Morgan there?'

'No, I've phoned all the places I can think of. . .' Rita began.

'I can't get an ambulance, so I'm going to try

and get Ben to hospital myself,' Dempsey told her.

There was a moment's pause at the other end of the line, then Bart's voice, crisp and businesslike.

'Dempsey, it's Bart. What's the problem?'

Somehow Dempsey wasn't surprised to hear him.

'I think Ben Marston has meningitis. He's got a pyrexia of forty, heart-rate of a hundred and sixty, can barely breathe, and I'm not even sure if he's conscious. He had a severe photophobia when I arrived, couldn't face the light at all, but now I can't get any response from him. Because of a road accident and traffic jam, the ambulance can't get through.' An unprofessional wobble crept into her voice. 'I'm going to try and drive him to the hospital myself.'

'Can you get him to the open ground by the village hall?'

'I should think so.'

'Take him there in your car. I'll be with you in five minutes.'

'Come on, Mrs Marston.' Dempsey slammed down the receiver and almost ran into the bedroom.

It's amazing, she thought, that, even though I hate the idea of seeing him again, at any hint of trouble he makes me feel so safe.

Carefully she dressed Ben in his bright red dressing-gown, wrapped him in the duvet and picked him up.

'Bring my medical bag and come with me.' Hoping that her bossiness was keeping Mrs

Marston calm, Dempsey went awkwardly along the path to her car. Although normally he wasn't heavy, now, in his unconscious state, Ben's weight pulled at her arms, but soon she had him in the back seat, his head resting on his mother's lap.

The road was mercifully clear, and they reached the field beside the village hall just as a noisy clatter above them warned of a helicopter's approach.

Almost before it landed, Bart jumped down, raced across the grass and took Ben from his mother's arms.

'We're going to the Cornish General. There's a helicopter landing area there, and it'll save a lot of time in the long run.' Shouting the words above the noise of the engine, Bart lifted Ben, then quickly clambered back inside the helicopter and he and the pilot waved as the giant metal insect lifted, then swooped away, the last sight of it through the clouds being the distinctive 'S.E.' logo.

He looked pale, Dempsey thought. Even behind the dark glasses, his face was drawn. She didn't stop to wonder at the fact of Bart being there exactly when he was needed. It seemed so like him, to come down literally from the clouds and deal with her worries. But I mustn't think about him—I mustn't, she told herself.

She dragged her mind away and, with a sigh of relief, ushered Mrs Marston into the car.

'Come on, let's go, and perhaps you could make

me a cup of coffee while I ring the surgery and tell
Rita what's happening.'

'Do you think he'll live?' Ben's mother whispered the words as Dempsey pulled away.

'If Dr Saville's got anything to do with it, he
will.' Dempsey patted the other woman's arm.
'There's no reason why Ben shouldn't make a
good recovery. Give it an hour and we'll ring the
hospital and find out more. In the meantime,
could you use some company? I'm exhausted after
all that tension, you must be too, and I'm going to
take an hour's break. I might as well wait with
you, if you don't mind.'

'I'd be very grateful to have you here.' Mrs
Marston opened her front door. 'I'll get us some
lunch. Would an omelette and salad be all right?'

Dempsey peeled off her dress and threw it on her
bed. Tutting impatiently, she went back to her
wardrobe and tossed one garment after another in
an untidy heap.

'I've got nothing fit to wear,' she moaned to
herself. 'Everything looks terrible.'

Apart from her gold dress, which she'd worn to
Bart's party, and which she felt she would never
want to wear again, everything she owned
seemed somehow dowdy.

Just when I want to make a big impression, she
thought. A glance at the clock told her that she
hadn't any more time to waste, and in desperation
she picked a silky top and skirt in shades of tan
and orange. She was beginning to think that

accepting the Morgans' invitation was a mistake. If Bart really was going. . .

Since his dramatic re-entry into her life when he'd taken Ben to hospital, Dempsey had only seen him once.

Arriving early one morning at the surgery, she had bumped into him as he appeared from Dr Morgan's office, and he'd walked past without speaking, just a nod in her direction as he left.

Now she'd been issued with an almost royal command to dinner by David and Mary, David telling her that he had important matters to discuss about the practice.

With a final tug at her hair, Dempsey ran from the flat and drove quickly to the Morgans' lovely old farmhouse. Her fluster about getting ready had been unnecessary, for she was the first to arrive.

'Come and sit down.' David ushered her into the living-room, with its old-fashioned but comfortable armchairs and softly polished wood, passing her a glass of sherry.

'I thought you might like to know I've seen Ben today. He's looking much better. Thank goodness they didn't have to intubate him—I think the fright of seeing him on a ventilator would have finished his mother completely.' David took a swallow from his glass.

'She's coped very well, though, hasn't she? I can't decide whether this will make her more or less anxious in the future,' Dempsey remarked.

'We'll have to wait and see.' He sat back and stretched his legs out in front of him. 'Still, it could have been a very different story if Bart hadn't been there.'

'Someone taking my name in vain?' Dempsey sat bolt upright, her heart beating painfully fast. She hadn't heard Bart's arrival, and the unexpected sight of him, as he strolled into the room, brought back all her longing. He stood by the fireplace, one hand resting on the mantel. Dressed in a light grey suit, with a striped shirt and dark grey tie, he was the picture of easy casual elegance.

'Hello, Bart. What can I get you to drink?' Quickly David jumped to his feet and hurried to the sideboard.

'Scotch, with a little water, if you have it. Thanks.'

'We were just saying it was lucky you were around when Ben was so ill the other day. The story might not have turned out so happily otherwise.'

Bart shrugged and sipped at his drink. 'I only did what anyone would have done in the circumstances.'

'Well——' David laughed '—I tell you now, you have a very big fan in Ben's mother. She thinks you're the best thing that's ever happened in Penmawtha.'

'Glad someone appreciates me.' Not looking in Dempsey's direction, Bart crossed the room and sat opposite her, an ankle resting on the opposite knee, his hands clasped around it.

'You're very quiet tonight, Dempsey. Let me get you another.' Her host reached for her glass.

'No more for me, thank you, David.'

'Well, in that case, I'll see how Mary's getting on in the kitchen.'

'I'll come with you.' Hastily Dempsey stood up and went to follow David, but he pushed her gently back into the chair and disappeared.

'Thank you for helping with Ben the way you did,' she said.

Bart inclined his head without speaking, then sipped at his drink.

In an agony of nervous tension, Dempsey hugged her glass to her. This was far worse than she'd expected. Why on earth didn't he say something, ask her something, mention her hurried departure? If he wouldn't, she must.

'I expect you're——' But she was interrupted by the welcome sound of Rita's cheerful voice, as her friend flung back the door to announce that dinner was ready.

'Great,' sighed Dempsey. She'd been reprieved for the moment.

'Frank can't make it,' Rita told her as they sat down in the kitchen round the big wooden table. Dempsey tried to take a place well away from Bart, but it wasn't to be. She sat quietly, trying to ignore the occasional pressure of his arm and the sensation of his nearness that seemed to burn into her.

Once in the company of the others, he burst into sparkling form, regaling them with a fund of amusing anecdotes, telling them of bizarre incidents in his research work, flirting lightly with Rita and Mary. But every time he looked towards

Dempsey, though he was always polite, his eyes were so devoid of expression that they looked like hollows set in his face.

'Would anyone like a drop of port?' The plates were cleared and David brought out a cheeseboard and some celery. 'No one? That's a shame. I've a very nice old tawny; never mind. Perhaps we'd better get down to business.' He raised an eyebrow in Mary's direction and she nodded.

'We've asked you here because what we have to say will affect all of you.'

'That sounds ominous.' Dempsey blinked and sipped at her coffee.

'You know that Jenny was involved in a car accident and injured her spine?'

Everyone nodded.

'You also probably know that she hasn't severed the spinal cord, merely has a contusion, so her chances of recovery are very good, thank God——'

'Get on with it, love,' Mary interrupted.

'Well, to cut a long story short, Mary and I are thinking of going to live in Cardiff for the next year to look after Jenny. She wants to try and continue with her studies and also be with her friends.' Dempsey knew what was coming next. Oh, no, she thought, oh, no! How could you do this to me, David, how could you?

'Well, it couldn't have worked out better in some ways. Bart wants to stay here for a while, and is very happy to take over the practice for me.'

'I don't think that's——' Dempsey pulled herself up from her chair, but was pushed back by Bart before she could say any more.

'I think it could work out very well for all of us,' he cut in smoothly. 'With Dempsey and Rita to help me, you need have no worries about the patients, and I already feel at home in the village.'

'And, of course, you'll be right on the spot for the development,' Dempsey said sharply.

'Haven't you heard?' David looked at her in surprise.

'We're not going through with it,' Bart said quietly.

'You're not?' Dempsey shrieked. 'Oh, that's wonderful!' Without thinking, she flung her arms round Bart's neck, almost crying. 'Oh, thank you, Bart, thank you.' Planting noisy kisses on his face, she didn't notice the stunned expressions on the faces of the others.

'Well, Dempsey, much as I hate to stop this demonstration of emotion, the reason we couldn't continue was the old mine workings in the area. Your "Foggy" subterranean galleries are everywhere, and the foundations would have been prohibitively expensive and, even then, not very safe.'

Crimson with embarrassment, Dempsey sank into her seat. What a fool she was. Fancy thinking that Bart and his father would be swayed by anything other than business considerations.

'Sorry to have made so much fuss. If you'll excuse me, I'll make a move.' Barely pausing to say goodnight, she rushed from the room, her face burning, her eyes full of angry tears.

'I must be stupid; fancy letting myself go like that.' She leaned against the gatepost and wiped her eyes with a tissue. 'Well, Dempsey, that'll teach you not to take anything for granted.'

'Are you all right?' She hadn't heard Bart's approach. He's as light-footed as a cat, she thought.

'I'm fine, Dr Saville, I'm fine. What do you think?' she said bitterly. 'I've had a wonderful evening. I have to work with someone that I hoped I'd never see again, I jump to conclusions and make an absolute fool of myself, and I feel wretched,' she wailed.

'Dempsey, Miss Dempsey, please don't cry. Dempsey, don't. I can't bear it if you're unhappy.' Gently lifting her chin, Bart thumbed away the tears on her cheek, then bent and kissed each side of her face.

'Why did you run away?' he whispered softly, punctuating his words with tiny kisses over her face and neck.

'I told you, in my note. Don't keep doing that; I can't think. . .'

'What you wrote in the note was, as our American cousins say, garbage.' Gently he nibbled her ear.

'All right; I heard you and your father talking that morning. You said you were marrying me to get the development through.'

'I did what?' Bart stood back and stared at her, open-mouthed.

'You said, or your father said, that if I was your

wife it would be more difficult for me to oppose the development.'

Bart frowned. 'And you thought that was why I wanted to marry you?'

'Well, you didn't say you loved me, and in the world of big business, which I know nothing about, it could be a good enough reason.'

'So you want me to tell you I love you? Don't you think friendship is a firm enough basis for marriage?' His arms around her waist, he studied her intently in the dim glow from the porch light.

'It's all right if both feel only friendship, but if one loves and the other doesn't. . .'

'And who do you think is the one with the love in this twosome?' demanded Bart.

Too late, Dempsey realised the mistake she'd made.

'I didn't say. . .' she began.

'Dempsey, tell me truthfully; do you love me?'

'I—er—er——' she stammered.

'All right, I'll start.' Bart moved away into the shadow, leaning one shoulder against the wall. 'Dempsey, Miss Dempsey, will you marry me? I think I fell in love with you the first time I saw you in that ridiculous hat, and I was sure of it when you stood up to us, my father and me, even though you were scared, at the meeting. You're funny, bright, sexy, have integrity, and I can't imagine a future without you.'

'Oh, Bart.' Dempsey rushed to him and fell into his arms.

'Does that mean yes?' he asked huskily.

'Yes, of course; I love you as much as it's

possible——'He pulled her close and kissed her trembling mouth, stilling the flow of words. Silently they clung, mouth to mouth, body to body, straining against one another until Dempsey thought she would drown in the sensation of their kiss.

'We'd better go and tell the others.' Shyly, she pulled away and looked into Bart's face. 'Did you ever suspect? About how I felt?'

'Well, I did wonder when I got your message that you were leaving.' He shook her shoulders. 'Don't you ever do that to me again, do you understand?'

Wordlessly, Dempsey shook her head. Then, in a puzzled tone, 'You said you wondered about how I felt?'

'Oh, yes. The message you wrote was on the back of the card I sent, when I first asked you out. I tried to comfort myself with the thought that if you'd kept it all that time it might mean something. It was the only thing that gave me hope.'

'I still can't believe it. Tell me again, please, why you love me.'

'You're fishing, aren't you?' Bart teased. 'Come closer,' he whispered. Gently he nibbled her lower lip. 'As I've told you before, I can't resist such a lovely mouth.' Then, as one, arms entwined around one another, they walked back inside.

— *MEDICAL ROMANCE* —

The books for enjoyment this month are:

DEMPSEY'S DILEMMA Christine Adams
WIND OF CHANGE Clare Lavenham
DOCTOR ON SKYE Margaret O'Neill
CROSSROADS OF THE HEART Judith Worthy

♥ ♥ ♥ ♥ ♥

Treats in store!

Watch next month for the following absorbing stories:

SAVING DR GREGORY Caroline Anderson
FOR LOVE'S SAKE ONLY Margaret Barker
THE WRONG DIAGNOSIS Drusilla Douglas
ENCOUNTER WITH A SURGEON Janet Ferguson

Available from Boots, Martins, John Menzies, W.H. Smith, most supermarkets and other paperback stockists.

Also available from Mills & Boon Reader Service, P.O. Box 236, Thornton Road, Croydon, Surrey CR9 3RU.

Readers in South Africa - write to:
Book Services International Ltd, P.O. Box 41654, Craighall, Transvaal 2024.